Books by Jaime Samms and Sarah Masters

The Dreaming

Tools of Justice
Tools of Change

Single Titles

Nurture

Books by Sarah Masters

Voices

Needing
Wanting
Keeping
Aching
Faking
Hiding
Taking
Leaving

Anthologies

Aim High
I Need a Hero

Single Titles

Outcast Cowboys
Empathy for a Killer

Books by Jaime Samms

Tales from Rainbow Alley

Finders, Keepers
Fix This, Sir
Face to Face
Neat Trick

Anthologies

Saddle Up 'N Ride

Nurture

ISBN # 978-1-78686-153-5

Cover Art by Posh Gosh ©Copyright 2017

Interior text design by Claire Siemaszkiewicz

Pride Publishing

NURTURE

SARAH MASTERS
&
JAIME SAMMS

Dedication

Always for Sarah who loves to lead me to the dark side
while I pretend to resist. ~Jaime
Muhahahaha ~ Sarah

Chapter One

Khakis, sandals and a long-sleeved white tee, and those incredible dark eyes locking with mine as the car stopped, eclipsed everything else in the park. His suggestive smile went straight to my dick. The guy on the path beside the car was built, and even the smoke billowing from between his lips didn't deter my appetite for the cut of his abdomen under his tight top, the way the white contrasted with his dark skin, or the round, neat swell of his ass.

Beside me in the car, Carl scowled at the red light through the windshield. "You're cruising him!"

"Oh fuck, please. I'm looking out the window."

"But you think he's hot."

The park, and the stud, slid away on my right while Carl pulled through the intersection.

"So? So do you." The pathetic little statement squished itself out through my teeth. I hated when he was right, when his anger was justified.

He jerked the car violently around the corner. "I wouldn't say so to my boyfriend, though, Paul." Tires squealed as he hammered the gas.

I gripped the door handle and pursed my lips. "No. You'd come back here later, when I'm sleeping, and fuck him in some dark alley."

"Shithead." He braked hard, and the tire jumped the curb outside my building.

I opened the door then thrust one foot out and looked back at him. "You coming up?"

He threw the car into park then slammed his way out and up to the apartment where a few minutes later he shoved me against the closing door. His lips, hard and demanding on my mouth, weren't offering romance or pleasure. He wasn't offering anything, only taking exactly what he wanted.

I don't know if you could ever have called what Carl and I did together 'making love'. I knew lately the barely concealed violence behind his every touch was getting to be too much, even for my tastes. After the guy-in-the-park argument, he'd dispensed with hiding the aggression altogether. I had to steam the ache out of my back for hours in a hot bath once he'd left.

I vowed, as I sat on the fire escape later and rubbed liniment onto my chafed wrists, I was never letting him in the door again.

A month ago, smoke and the taste of ash and cancer would have kept me company out here. Tonight, not even starlight struggled through the city smog and overcast sky. The sounds of traffic drifted up from the street. I listened to the city's song for a while, wondering when it had replaced birdsong in my mind as comfort music. It *was* comforting, though. It filled the void that got bigger every time Carl—

"Shit." I needed a smoke. Instead, I twisted the lid back on the tube of cream and leaned my head on the rail. My wrists stung. I'd told him the restraints were too tight, and he'd laughed. I should never have invited him up. Not when he was mad. There was nothing left. He was violent and angry and dangerous, and one of these days he was really going to hurt me. I wouldn't be able to stop him.

"Idiot." I tangled my fingers in my hair, tried again to convince myself. I needed to get rid of him. So why did I listen so hard for the door, for his knock? Why did I sit out there waiting for him to come back, flowers in hand, and tell me how sorry he was?

I shifted, maneuvering for a more relaxing position on the hard metal step. My ribs complained. There would be bruises. I'd have to call my friend Brian and beg off the swim practice tomorrow. I wasn't interested in fielding the looks or coming up with another plausible excuse.

The knock came just as the breeze picked up, carrying the shrill wail of a siren down the alley. I scrabbled inside then slammed the window down. Drops of rain plopped against the glass, and in a moment, a torrent flooded the streets. I fully expected to find Carl on the other side of the door.

"Hey." Brian stood there, hands stuffed in his pockets. "I saw Carl's car. It's gone now."

I clenched my teeth around disappointment I shouldn't feel. "Yeah. He left."

I backed away from the entrance, leaving it open. Brian shambled in, closing the door in his wake. I had my back to him, so when he grabbed my arm, I jumped and jerked away.

"You put something on that?" he asked, lifting my wrist to show the redness.

"What do you want, Bri?"

A heavy sigh tickled the back of my neck.

"You coming to the pool tomorrow?" He said it like he already knew the answer, so I didn't bother responding. "Let me see."

"What?" I skidded off to one side at that, putting the table between us. "See what?"

"The bruises. How bad?" He just assumed they were there. No question other than how bad.

"Not..." I shook my head, swallowed. He'd never asked *that* before. "He's probably going to be back soon. You should—"

Someone knocked. For a second, we both turned to the sound, neither of us moving.

"What's he going to do?" Brian asked.

"Nothing."

"Paul—"

"Nothing! He'll apologize. Hang out a bit. Then he'll go home."

"Why do you let him do this?"

"Oh, please." I stalked around the table, keeping him

on the other side, then reached for the door handle. "Like you've never had a bit of rough sex in your life. That Denis guy—"

"Never made me feel like I should be making excuses for him."

I said nothing, but I didn't open the door, either.

"Denis never did anything we didn't agree on beforehand, Paul," he said, suggesting, too accurately, that maybe Carl crossed that particular line.

"Not having this conversation, Brian. I'm going to let him in, and you're going to leave."

Brian shook his head, his jaw tight, his eyes blazing, but I yanked the door open before he could say anything. Carl's smile flashed bright, momentarily blinding my good sense, like it always did. Brian glared at him as he squeezed past, and for one split second, the expressions on both of their faces made the growing storm outside seem tame. Then Brian had gone, and Carl was filling the tiny apartment with his presence.

"What the fuck did he want?" Carl asked, shoving Paul's chest and sending him sprawling backward against the hallway wall.

Paul stared at him, mouth an O, hazel eyes wide as if he had something to hide. Well, Carl would soon get it out of him if he did. No way was he letting Paul bullshit him with tales of Brian popping round to check if they were going swimming. Fucking swimming! If he ever found out it was more than that, he'd—

"He came round to ask about swimming." Paul straightened up, darting his eyes toward the front door.

Jesus Christ...

"Swimming. Right. And you expect me to believe that, do you? Get in there." Carl pointed in the direction of the bedroom—his heart thudding dully—and bunched his fists.

Paul moved off the wall. He walked into the room, waiting

just inside the doorway. "I... Carl, I'm not —"

"Not what? Not in the mood? Not telling the truth again?" Carl smirked, trailing his fingers down Paul's cheek. "You know you're in the mood. Now get on the bed."

Paul did as asked, his movements sluggish, and he winced once or twice when settling back onto the mattress.

"What's the matter, Paul?" Carl stood at the foot of the bed studying the man he enjoyed tormenting. Paul enjoyed it too, he was sure of that. He just needed a little encouragement to admit it, that was all.

"Nothing."

"Good."

Carl strode to the wardrobe. He pulled out a hanger holding Paul's belts then selected a wide leather one for maximum pleasure-pain. At the side of the bed, he held Paul's wrists together with one large hand so he could wind the thick belt around them. He secured the buckle, and Paul stared up at him, the pain from his already chafed wrists apparent.

"You know pain is part of the game, so quit complaining inside that damn head of yours," Carl said. "Accept it, and you'll enjoy it more. I've told you this before." He hauled Paul up the mattress, closer to the headboard, and reached to the bedside cabinet for a silk scarf. After looping it through the tiny gap between Paul's wrists, he threaded one end of the scarf around the iron bed strut and tied it to the other. "And as I've also told you before, you can transcend the pain if you put your mind to it. You've never yet reached that heightened state, have you?" He shook his head and rifled in the drawer for the lube. "Shit, you're missing out."

Carl dropped the tube on the bed, straddling Paul while gripping the neck of his T-shirt. He ripped it down the middle. Chest exposed, Paul lay still and unresponsive — save for watching Carl as though he hated him.

I wonder if he does?

Carl shrugged, not giving a shit either way, and moved down Paul's body, popping open his jeans button and tugging at the zipper. He yanked the jeans away then tossed them to the floor to get at the boxers he'd repeatedly asked Paul not to wear.

"Why do you keep defying me?" Carl mused.

Paul didn't answer.

"If you don't answer, I'll get pissed, and when I get pissed, you know what happens, don't you?"

Paul nodded. "I, uh, I forgot."

"You forgot. Right. Okay."

Carl got off the bed. He returned to the wardrobe to pull out a whippet-thin black belt. He spun then lunged toward the bed and raised his arm. The belt cracked across Paul's chest, and his torso rose, arm muscles bulging, neck tendons corded, pressing against the skin. Paul dropped back down to the mattress, and damn, that man never uttered a fucking word.

He'll regret that.

"You won't forget again, will you?" Carl climbed on the bed. He kneeled between Paul's legs and took out his own cock. He settled his lover's ass on his thighs.

Paul shook his head, and Carl had the fleeting thought of whether it was a response to his question or his way of saying he didn't want Carl doing what he was about to.

Doesn't matter what he means. He should have obeyed. Now, he can put up and shut the fuck up.

He lubed his dick and, without priming the hole, spread Paul's ass cleft and settled his cock tip against that pucker he loved so much. He glanced up. Paul widened his eyes, and he bit his lower lip.

"You like this, huh, Paul? Yeah, you do."

He eased his dick inside, smug that Paul's cock hardened and bobbed. Usually, he took his time, stretching Paul slowly, but now? Seeing Brian here had pissed him off. Knowing Paul didn't care enough about his rules to even remember them was worse. Paul was going to take it how it came. Fuck the burn.

Carl began a swift rhythm, short, sharp thrusts that

turned him on so much he almost came right then. Seeing Paul bound and at his mercy always did that. No one else had ever made him feel the way this man did. He worked harder, faster, and his bollocks tautened as release came too close.

"Come," he said through clenched teeth. "Come, Paul."

Carl closed his eyes and spewed cum, the rush of orgasm heady, almost too much to handle. He pumped again and again, releasing all he had to give, then slowed and opened his eyes. Paul's stomach remained dry, and his cock had started to soften right along with Carl's.

"You didn't come." Statement, not a question.

Paul shook his head.

Carl pulled out then got off the bed. In the bathroom, he washed his cock with irate, soapy strokes. The *asshole*. He returned to the bedroom to glare at his disrespectful lover. "Why didn't you come?"

Paul closed his eyes for a moment. Once he opened them again, he stared at Carl with…defiance?

"You've fucked me off, you know that?" He smacked a fist into Paul's gut. Paul's knees rose, and a muffled "Oomph!" came out from between partially open lips.

"I'm going to leave you there like that for a while. All tied up. I'll take your keys and come back when I think you deserve to be released. You got that?"

Paul nodded.

Carl left the apartment, anger blazing a trail through his chest. He swallowed bile and got into his car, intent on hitting a bar or two and seeing where the night took him. He'd see to Paul another time, maybe tomorrow, catch him unawares, teach him a lesson. No way was he going to put up with that crap. He called the shots, not Paul.

He drove to town, bringing the car to a screeching halt in a side street. Out on the sidewalk, he slammed the door and clicked the lock button on his key fob. The rain had stopped, thank God, and he walked to the town proper. Throbbing beats filtered from the pubs he passed, but Dewer's and

The Anchor didn't appeal. No, he was headed for Jilly's Club, the place where like-minded people got trashed and went home to fuck and strive for sexual peaks they'd never reached before.

His cock hardened at the thought.

Once there, he approached the head of the line, ignoring the straggle of drunkards waiting patiently to get in. The bouncer nodded at him and opened the door, and Carl breezed inside like he owned the joint. At the bar, impatience ripped through him, and he rapped on the wooden surface. A barmaid studied him, eyes narrowed, her glare telling him she thought of him as a cocksucker.

She's got that right.

He smirked and waited for her to give in and serve him. She did.

Carl paid her then walked off sipping from his beer bottle, searching out a potential guy for what he had in mind. He spotted him in the corner, the man already too drunk to stand straight, all spiked-up hair and muscles. Not Carl's usual fare, but it didn't matter what a one-night stand looked like. Carl neared him, watched as the guy stood straighter and puffed out his chest.

Placing his bottle on a nearby table, Carl asked, "You want something?" He glanced down at his crotch then back to the man's.

"Yeah. You?"

"Yeah. Come on." Carl jerked his head in the direction of the club's rear and walked away, confident the man would follow.

When he reached the back fire escape door, he leaned against it, pleased that his next fuck arrived at his side. Carl surveyed the area. No one paid them any attention, so he pushed down on the metal bar. The door swung open, and Carl stepped outside, beckoning the man to follow.

"You like it *outside*?" Spiked Hair asked.

"Yeah. Shut the door and come with me."

Carl walked close to the building, knowing exactly where

the security cameras were from the last time he'd done this. He strode along the wet backstreet then turned down a side alley, smiling to himself upon hearing heavy pursuing footsteps. He stopped halfway behind some large refuse bins and waited.

"Here?" his companion asked.

"Yeah, here." Carl nodded. "Lean up against the wall. I like it there. Face it."

Spiked Hair did, and despite the dimness, Carl made out that tight ass and thick thighs. He reached out a hand to grip the man's hair.

"You like it rough?" Carl asked, pulling Spiked Hair's head back.

"Yeah. Some."

"Good." Carl slipped his free hand inside his jacket pocket then brought out a knife. He raised it. Eased the blade in the space between the man's neck and the wall, and drew it across his skin in a quick, sharp movement. "As rough as that?" he whispered, holding the man's weight as he sagged and struggled to speak. "Fucking prick."

Carl stepped back, let the man go, and watched him fall to the ground. Anger assuaged, he left the alley, peering down at his clothes when he passed under a streetlight. Not a speck of blood that he could see.

Damn, he was getting good at this shit.

Chapter Two

"Fucker." Not nearly enough venom laced the word, but I could barely breathe, let alone spit vitriol. It roiled inside me, though, made my stomach lurch and spin at the thought of coming with that asshole inside me. I was done. Nothing he could say could make up for this one. The need to puke forced me to ignore the pain and squirm up until I could get my teeth at the knot in the scarf.

Transcend the pain, my ass. I took a few gasping breaths, hoped Carl hadn't cracked one of my ribs, then sank my teeth into the silk. I almost had it tugged loose.

A key rattled in the door.

Already?

"Shit."

Amazing how the sound of a key in a lock could be so loud. For a split second, I hated myself for the way I scrambled back down flat on my back on the bed like a frightened puppy, tired of getting kicked. Then the ache of the awkward movements spread through my ribs and stomach, and the residual burn of the lash across my chest let me convince myself there was nothing wrong with self-preservation.

I clamped my lips around the urge to tell him to fuck off, to leave me alone. He wanted me to speak up, wanted to hear my anger. It turned him on. I wasn't about to give him the satisfaction. I stared up at the ceiling as the apartment door opened and footsteps clomped through the entry. Never mind the way my heart raced, pounding against sore ribs from the inside. Never mind the cold sweat. Fuck. I wasn't afraid of the fucker.

"Paul? Dude, you still here?"

Brian. Perfect. I kicked at the sheets, trying to hook them and draw them up with my toes. The bed creaked under my shifting weight.

"I saw Carl's car leave. Just wanted to… Jesus."

If I thought I'd felt sick before, now I didn't think I could speak without hurling.

"See you're okay," he finished, his voice low and shaking, skimming the edge of fury.

I looked away, clamping my teeth down on the sick as he strode across the room to kneel on the bed. He had me loose in a few seconds, and I bolted for the bathroom, slamming the door behind me.

I didn't lock it, though. I should have. He came in as I was still leaning over the toilet, wiping my mouth with the back of my hand.

"Paul—"

"Don't." I reached and pulled away my torn shirt. I tossed it into the trash and thought about getting up.

Brian touched my shoulder, but I slid away, getting to my feet and snatching up a pair of jeans hanging over the edge of the vanity. I didn't bother with underwear. Oh, the irony.

"He left you tied up," Brian said.

"No shit." I shouldered past him. Grabbed a tank top from the floor to throw over the evidence of what else Carl had done to me. "There's a duffel on the shelf in the closet." I yanked open the dresser drawer so I could gather up all the clean underwear and socks, then moved to the next for T-shirts.

Brian had the duffel out by then and tossed it onto the bed for me to fill. I grabbed everything I thought I might need for the next few days, stuffing a few suits haphazardly into a garment bag and shoes and jeans into the duffel.

"Um…you do realize this is your apartment?" Brian said.

He was in the bathroom, dropping hair gel and my toothbrush into a toiletry bag, though, and I silently thanked him for understanding. My apartment, maybe. My happy place? Not even close. Not anymore.

"He'll be back," I said. "Sooner or later. And he knows exactly how long he has to stay away for me to forgive him."

"Forgive him?" Now Brian stopped helping me pack to stare at me from the bathroom, though, going by the weight of that stare, he might as well have been standing over me. "This isn't just rough sex anymore, Paul."

I tightened my jaw so much it ached, and I had to wiggle it loose before I could speak. "I don't need you to tell me what this is, thank you very much."

"It's fucked up, is what it is," he muttered.

I wondered if he thought I couldn't hear him.

"Asshole," he said.

He glanced at me but thankfully didn't say anything. I didn't exactly need him to tell me I was being a jerk. He just handed me the bag, and I threw it on top of everything else in the duffel then zipped it up. I slung the handle over my shoulder.

"That everything?" he asked.

A heavy sigh escaped, and I shook my head. "Probably not. Come on." I hauled my stuff out to the entry where I opened the drawer of the hall table. "Fucker!"

"What?" Brian peered over my shoulder into the empty space.

"He took my wallet." I slammed the drawer, and the front clattered to the floor under the force of my fury. I'd planned on finding a nice, anonymous hotel where he couldn't find me. Without my credit cards or ID on a Saturday night, I didn't have access to my money until I could replace them on Monday. He was probably racking up my bill as I stood there cursing him.

"Bri?"

"Yeah. Come on. You can sleep on the couch." He clapped me on the back and sighed. "I'm sure Lil will have something to say about it. You ready for that?"

"Lillian can stuff his fat cock up in his big girl panties and suck it up."

"Hey!"

Brian stepped back, but not before I felt the vibration of his anger in the air. It was a vibe I knew intimately and shied away from.

"Sorry." It had been a nasty thing to say. "Carl's crap rubs off on me sometimes."

"Well, take a fucking hot shower and scrub it off, because Lil takes enough of that from people we don't call friends, and if you piss us off, you can take your chances with the asshole."

I nodded. "I'm sorry."

"You're my best friend, Paul, and this is a shitty place to be in, but I won't choose you over Lil. Don't make me."

"I know. I won't."

The last thing I needed was to piss Brian off. He was helping me, and even though he and Lil had gone through some nasty shit, they were solid now. I didn't have to like the guy who'd made Brian's life hell for so long, but I didn't have a right to judge him, either.

We walked to his car in silence. Brian had a right to be annoyed, and I wasn't in the mood to make him feel better, even if it was my fault. He lived closer to the bar district than I did and had to drive around the block a few times before he found a parking spot close enough to his apartment to satisfy him. The quiet had lost most of its strain by the time he'd killed the engine.

He dropped his hands from the wheel and turned a bit to face me. "I get it, you know. How you feel about Lil. All the fights and drinking, and everything else, and I know there was a lot you had to watch me put up with. I know why you don't like my lover. Especially now, with Carl, I get it. But Lil isn't a man like Carl. There was a lot of shit we went through, a lot of soul searching, and not all of it was constructive, but the search is over. Lil's happy now. We're happy."

I nodded. His little speech wasn't meant to rub in my

idiocy, or my mistakes in keeping Carl around for so long. He wasn't trying to fuel my anger. It just worked out that way.

After a minute, when I didn't say anything, he sighed and got out of the car. I only hesitated a second before following him. Where else was I going to go?

I wasn't even inside before Lil was there, pulling Brian in the door and wrapping him up in a greedy embrace.

"Where the hell have you been?" Lil asked.

His voice was tight and hard, and I couldn't help but flinch at his unveiled emotion. Demonstrative didn't begin to describe Lil. When he noticed me, the light in his eyes went from fierce to cold, and I instinctively backed against the closed door.

"Who let him and his issues in here?" Lil sniped.

"Nice to see you, too, pot," I muttered, angry at myself for how easily a big man could intimidate me, even without meaning to. It never used to be my default, and Lil wasn't even huge. He was tall, sure, willow-thin and sculpted, probably strong as an ox, but for all his vices over the years, one thing he'd never done was raise a finger against anyone.

I pushed past them as Lil gently set Brian aside and turned to me.

"Don't get comfy, sugar. I don't know why you're here, but you can bet your silly, bruised little bottom you are *not* staying."

One probably couldn't die of a tongue lashing, but Lil never got tired of trying to flail me. This time, the too-accurate jibe hurt. Damned if I was going to let him know that. I sneered.

"Lil, please—" Brian put a hand on Lil's arm.

Lil shook him off. "He's only going to go back, Bri. How many times you gonna save him before you understand? He doesn't want to be saved."

"What would you know about it?" I shot back.

"I know if you had any balls," Lil whispered, "you'd have hit him back."

"Rich, coming from the guy in the skirt." I fumbled with the strap of my duffel. I'd slung it across my chest, and the quick motions of trying to get rid of it reminded me exactly why I was not going back. "I don't need saving. I certainly won't be hiding under your petticoats."

"No. Nothing to tie you up with under there."

"Guys!" Brian stepped up, finally, shot a look at Lil, who glared, and Brian softened. "People. Please. He left, Lil. Do you get it? He left. Even you have to support that move."

Lil tightened his lips to a thin line, but he gave a curt nod. "Fine." He shifted his weight and the slight lean toward Brian drew his lover a few steps closer, into his orbit. "He can stay, but I don't have to like it."

Brian smiled at him, and he calmed, touched Brian's cheek and nodded his acceptance.

The grin Brian flashed at his lover sent a white-hot flare of jealously that spiked my heart rate.

Then Brian was turning to me. "Take your coat off, Paul. I'll see if I can find something to eat."

"I'm not hungry." I did remove my jacket, though, and tossed it on the chair.

Lil grunted, curled his lip, and stared at my jacket pointedly, crossing his arms over his chest. I reached to pick it up again. It wasn't worth listening to him bitch.

"Well, shit, honey. Don't those bruises go deep."

Lil stopped my reach by grabbing my wrist. I tried to twist away, but he held tight. He was strong, and damn it if the panic didn't set in and I strained a little harder.

"That goes beyond a little chafing, honey," he said.

"I am not your honey." I managed to yank free and grabbed up my coat, hugging it to my chest and feeling like a fool.

"But he is a nurse, Paul. Let him clean you up."

"I don't need —"

Lil's hand on my wrist, just above the raw, painful skin, stopped me talking. There was not a bit of force, more of a light touch, only two fingers that gave anger no target. Even

21

his voice was soft when he spoke. Nothing to be afraid of.

"Let someone be nice to you for a change, honey. I promise it feels way better than this shit."

"Someone like you?" But I couldn't muster anything more than petulance, and Lil didn't rise to that.

"Someone like a nurse," Lil said. "Why not?"

"Only if you stop calling me honey."

He actually smiled. "Sure thing, sugar. Get on in the bathroom. I have got to strip out of this get-up." He ran a hand down the front of his scrubs. "I won't be a minute."

In the bathroom, there was space. Blessed space, and no one in it but me. I sank onto a stool set in front of a tidy dressing table and mirror. It took a long time to get my breathing calm and my heart rate back to normal. I was tempted to just jump in the shower and let the hot water wash it all away, but a more careful study of the raw skin on my wrists made me think it might be better to let the professional do his thing.

He knocked before he came in and smiled at me. I recognized the nurse mask he'd put on despite the change into his own clothes. The veneer of polite care kept me calm. And, of course, he was right, and letting him wash me up and put ointment and bandages on the bleeding leather burn relaxed the tension some. I didn't even mind the pink leopard-print miniskirt so much. He had nice legs.

"It takes a lot of force to break the skin like this," he commented at one point.

It seemed like an obvious comment, so I didn't respond.

"He's escalating."

That made me look up, and I didn't expect the concern I saw in Lil's dark eyes. "Escalating?"

"I've been on the wrong end of a fist or two in my time, and more than one belonged to an aggressive boyfriend." He smiled, but it was a short, grim flash of bitter memory. "Who'd love a cross-dressing freak? I took what I could get. They put you in the hospital eventually, Paul. It doesn't get better."

"It does if you have Brian."

Now his smile was real, dazzling. "Then it does, yeah. Eventually. I didn't believe in him for a long time. People like Carl are easier to believe in, and that's sad."

I nodded. I couldn't not believe in Carl and his power to do anything when I saw the way the anger turned him. It was easy to want to believe I'd imagined the wild, the ugly, the terrifying. When he turned soft, when he apologized, that's what I wanted to be real. I couldn't deny the bruises or ignore the blood anymore, though.

"Guys?" Brian stuck his head in the doorway just as Lil was taping up the last bandage. "You should see this. It's happened again."

Lil stiffened, his fingers still and strong against the pulse on my wrist, but I could feel a tiny tremor run through him.

"It's all over the news," Brian went on.

"Where this time?" Lil's voice had gone flat.

I couldn't read the expression on his face, but that monotone, his controlled words, chilled me.

"Back of Jilly's."

"What are you guys talking about?" I knew Jilly's. I'd been there enough times before Carl had come along. I might even have met him there.

"You have to have had your head up your ass not to know," Lil snapped.

"Lil." Brian came in and put a hand on Lil's shoulder. "This is the first time it's even made the news. We know about the others because of Vic."

Lil nodded and pinched his lips. He took a deep breath then asked, "Was it anyone we know?"

"No idea." Brian looked grim. "Family notification first and all that. Vic will call."

"Who's Vic?" They might have forgotten I was there. Whatever they were talking about, it had turned them in on each other in their own brand of self-protection.

"Victor Bradley. He's a cop." Lil patted my wrist lightly and stood, the taffeta under his skirt rustling as he moved to the cabinet to stash away the first-aid kit. "My brother Jason was on the force. Vic was his work partner…"

His shoulders were stiff, straight, held like any sudden movement might break him. Brian watched him with worry.

"About eight months ago" — Lil's voice only carried because the hard tile surfaces didn't soak it up — "I called Jason. I wanted to talk to him. Would have been the first time in three years I saw him. He'd tossed me out on my ass, and I wanted him to know…" He sighed. "Wanted him to know I was cleaned up. Wanted him to meet Brian." A little glance at his lover shored him up a bit. "I should have gone to Jason's, but I thought The Anchor would be a safe, neutral space." He tightened his fingers around the sink bowl, and his breaths juddered.

Brian sidled close to him, just touched his fingers. "He was killed before we got there. No idea what happened. Just that we arrived, he wasn't there, and Lil was devastated. I brought Lil home, and an hour later, Vic shows up at the door, talking about murder. Jason stabbed seven times and left to bleed to death in an alley behind the club." He shook his head. "Someone walked away from that alley covered in blood, and they never even had a suspect."

Lil shook himself, straightened then turned. "The cops are still investigating, but Victor is convinced they'll never find the guy because they're ignoring important links they don't want to see. There have been four murders — five now with this new one tonight — and all of them gay victims. Well, all but Jason. He was just in the wrong place at the wrong time. He was only at The Anchor to meet me."

"So the police want a cop killer. But Vic's convinced this is something else entirely, and that his death is tied to the others. No one will listen to him. They think his death is about some case he worked, or some vendetta some criminal had against him," Brian added.

"No one seems to care that someone is luring gay men into filthy alleys to die," Lil said bitterly.

"Vic does." Brian ran a soothing hand down Lil's back. "He's doing his best."

Lil nodded, but his expression wasn't forgiving. "What kind of person does it take?" he wondered. "I was angry for a long time, at everything and everyone, and I don't get it. How much do you have to hate the world to do something like that? Over and over, like once couldn't possibly be enough?"

For all Lil sounded confused, Brian was the one who leaned on him, settling against his lanky form and under Lil's protective arm, and for the first time, I thought maybe I understood Lil. His drinking and his problems, even the skirts. The man knew who he was. It might have been a nightmare for him figuring himself out, but now he knew, and I suddenly understood how Brian found that attractive.

Chapter Three

Carl sat in his car and brooded. It hadn't taken long for the wail of sirens to split the air and the blue lights of police cars to slice through the darkness. Three cop cars had sped past him, and he'd put his head down as though searching in his glove box. Now, he stared ahead, spatters of rain plopping on the windshield, and turned his thoughts to Paul.

He'll be needing a piss right about now.

He laughed, loud and hearty, and covered his mouth with his hand. Biting down on the pad beneath his thumb to stop the laughter didn't work, so he gave it free rein until tears wet his cheeks. He ought to be getting back to Paul's really, but a ball of spite knotted hard in his gut. Who was he kidding? His relationship with Paul was all but over, yet he couldn't let him go. And if he did, he couldn't stand to let someone else touch him, need him, possess him.

Rage built inside Carl, and for the first time since he'd allowed himself to act on his violent urges, the need to kill again so soon goaded him. He usually went a while between murders, but tonight something had snapped. A new level had emerged—one that burned through him, bringing whispering voices that told him to take action now while the police were occupied with the latest body.

He thought of Paul pissing the bed and laughed again. Opening the car door so he could get out, he was careful to lock the vehicle behind him once on the sidewalk. He surveyed the area for any nosey bastards who might be watching. No one was about, so he walked toward town once again before stopping abruptly beneath a streetlight.

Tiny bloodstains marred his shirt.

I thought it hadn't splashed.

"Fuck!"

Carl ran back to his car. He opened the rear door then rifled through a holdall on the back seat. He pulled out a polo shirt he'd worn to play squash the other night then crouched behind the door to swap his clothing. The polo stank of sweat and the sport's club changing room, but he didn't give a shit. He stood to lean inside the car again, rooting about for his jacket. Once done up, it covered the shirt and all its wrinkles. He locked the car, pissed off at the wasted time, then walked to town, his pace quick, hands in his pockets.

As he strode past Jilly's, he smiled at his audacity.

The doorman was busy shouting at drunkards in the line outside. "You can't come in, all right? Place is closed."

A woman teetering on high heels, skirt showing her thonged ass, her hair a severe bob, staggered up to him. "But people are still in there. I can see them through the window."

"Everyone already in there has to stay in there until the police have finished taking their names and addresses. Look, I'm telling you, you're not getting in tonight."

"Asshole!" the woman shouted. Her knees jolted, and she grabbed a nearby man for support.

Carl sauntered past, chin to chest, and made his way to the end of the block then around the corner. The pink neon sign for Brewster's flashed, the glow hazy on the rain-slicked pavement. His excitement level increased, and he battled the urge to laugh again.

What the fuck is wrong with me?

Irked at his lack of self-control, he approached Brewster's. He peered through the window. Packed enough that his presence probably wouldn't be noted, the bar played a hit from the eighties that reminded Carl of summer days and hot sticky nights. He elbowed the door open then pushed through the crowd, heading for a guy nursing his pint of

Guinness in the far corner. Head down and foot tapping to the beat, the man looked out of his mind on booze.

Carl nudged him.

He raised his head to stare at Carl with glassy eyes.

"Do you, uh…?" Carl nodded at the drunkard's cock.

"Uh, have done, though I don't make a habit of it," he slurred, and one knee jerked. "Ah, fuck it. Yeah. Why not?"

"After you," Carl said, cocking his head in the direction of the door.

The dude necked back his drink then almost missed putting the glass on a small table. He weaved through customers, and Carl kept close behind, face lowered into his coat collar, eyes downcast.

Outside, Carl said, "Will the alley do you?"

Carl's prey nodded and took the lead, walking down the street in a wavy line. Carl followed, keeping to the shadows, and they reached an alley between two shops. The man disappeared into its mouth, and Carl glanced left then right before pursuing. Darkness seemed a tangible thing, oppressive and thick, and swallowed them whole. Carl tripped over debris and staggered forward, his curses heavy, echoing in the still air. His hands met with the man's back, and Carl patted him to get him to stop.

"Here," Carl said. "I can't wait. Up against the wall. Face it." He squinted, trying hard to make out his target's shape. Carl stepped up close. "You like it hard and fast?" His breaths left him in puffs, and he concentrated on forcing himself calm. "You like it like that, huh?" He imagined the guy nodding, and his cock hardened. Pulse thudding loud in his ears, Carl reached for the knife. With his free hand, he smoothed up and down his victim's back, creeping his fingers into his hair. Gripping it—God, he loved this bit— he yanked back the quarry's head and raised the blade, using his senses to guide him in the darkness.

"W-what's that?" the dude asked, trying to twist out of Carl's grasp.

"Just a little toy," Carl whispered, pressing it against a

soft neck that would gape open in seconds. He closed his eyes, savoring the throb of his cock for a moment, then drew the blade across.

Heat splattered his face, the copper stench of blood heady and arousing. Cum spurted in Carl's jeans, and he sagged with the man, body juddering, a whispered "Ah!" leaving his mouth. Heart beating hard, he dropped his kill and arced the blade downward, striking flesh by luck, not judgment. He hacked and stabbed, images of Paul tied to the bed seeping into his mind. Anger that Paul hadn't come on command ripped into him, and he raised the knife again and again, the blood on his face already drying, making his skin tight.

Bloodlust sated, he straightened up and slipped the knife back into his inside pocket. Cuffing his face, he hoped he'd wiped all the blood away. Realization slammed into him that if he didn't clean up, he'd draw attention to himself.

"Fucking shit!"

He made to turn and leave the alley, but a vicious thought struck him—one he couldn't resist obeying. Hand in jacket pocket, he withdrew Paul's wallet. Pulling down his polo shirt's hem, he covered his hand and flipped open the wallet, extracting one of Paul's credit cards.

"You didn't come," he said and tossed the card to the ground.

Wallet back in his pocket, he walked toward the alley's end, sloshing his feet through a puddle. He kneeled and scooped up as much water as he could and splashed his face, drying it with his damp sleeves. "Fucking teach you not to come."

At the end of the alley, he lowered his head a bit and gave the street a once-over, waiting while a gaggle of women exited Brewster's and tottered off up the road. He stepped out onto the sidewalk then walked back the way he had come, past Jilly's, now devoid of a queue, and headed for his car. Once seated inside, he repositioned the rear-view mirror so he could check out his face. He smiled at having cleaned off most of the blood.

"Fucking A!"

He gunned the engine then pulled away from the curb and took a right turn, intent on returning to Paul's and teaching him a damn lesson he'd never forget. Thoughts of what he'd do to him filled his mind on the journey, and he alternated between laughing and congratulating himself on his killing expertise.

Outside Paul's place, he parked. Locked up. Walked to the front door, fatigue overtaking him at an alarming rate. He let himself in then went into the kitchen to drink a cold beer, hoping it would wake him up before he went into the bedroom. The bubbles stung his throat, and he chuckled again at the irony.

Bet his throat stung... Bastard should have been more careful.

Beer gone, he dumped the bottle in the trash and made for the bedroom.

The door was closed.

I left it open...

He turned the handle and kicked the door open, filling the threshold to scare Paul with his appearance. The bed stood empty, the silk scarf resting on the rumpled sheets, and a burst of anger boiled in his gut.

"What the *fuck*?"

Though annoyed at himself for doing so, he crouched beside the bed and looked underneath. No one there. He stood then barged into the bathroom, noting Paul's jeans and a few toiletry items had gone. Carl stalked into the living room, heart thudding so painfully his chest hurt. His lungs felt as though someone squeezed them, and he struggled to inhale. Staring at the empty room, he clenched his teeth and fists, the backs of his eyes painful from the pressure growing inside his head.

He released a yell then quieted, mindful of the neighbors hearing him.

"Shit. Fucking *shit!*" he whispered.

Carl turned and reached the front door, his mind trying to

work out where Paul would have gone without his wallet.

Brian's? No, Lil doesn't like Paul. Who else would help him?

"Think!"

He yanked the door open and left the apartment, feet thumping on the ground, rage growing, festering. In his car, he started the engine, shoved into gear, then veered away from the curb calmly in case anyone watched.

The drive home was fraught with different scenarios. Carl coached himself to keep calm and deal with finding Paul in the morning — if the police hadn't picked the limp dick up before then. He grinned as he imagined how it would go. Cops finding the credit card and the body — and he had no doubt they'd find it tonight, what with door-to-door inquiries about the other jackass he'd killed. Paul being found and hauled in for questioning. Paul denying it, shitting bricks at being in trouble.

What did I see in him again?

He batted away the answer, not wanting to face up to the fact that Paul was good for him — *to* him. His relationship with Paul was the closest Carl had come to loving someone. Fucked if he could show it the way Paul wanted him to, though. Didn't Paul *see* Carl just wasn't *like* that? He needed the violence, the control. No way could he get down with any of the vanilla shit. And he thought Paul had liked the roughness too.

Unless he was lying. Or too damn weak to tell me where to get off.

But wasn't that what Carl wanted? Someone to bully?

"Damn fucking right!"

Carl parked on his driveway then leaned across to the back seat for his shirt. He sat for a moment, contemplating tonight's events. Shit, it seemed to have gone on forever. Seemed it had been hours ago that he'd fucked Paul. He peered at the dashboard clock. Just past ten.

"Jesus."

He left the car, locking it with the key fob as he walked away. Inside, he flicked on the hallway light. Moving to the large leather-framed mirror on the wall, he inspected his face. Flecks of dried blood smattered his hairline, and he reached up to pick some off. A flake stuck to his fingertip, and he brought it to his nose, sniffing heavily. It smelled of nothing. Disappointment thundered through him, and he studied his reflection, trying to see the person behind the mask. If he was honest, he couldn't find him — he'd lost himself too long ago to even remember what he used to be like.

Carl shrugged and took the stairs two at a time, going into the bathroom to set the shower on hot. He dropped his shirt to the floor then stripped, suddenly eager to wash away the filth of those men. The water burned his skin, but he gritted his teeth and scrubbed himself clean. Finished, he stepped out of the stall then dried his body, walking into the bedroom afterward to slip on some tracksuit bottoms.

"You never know, the police might be round at any time, asking if I know where Paul is."

His heart rate sped up. *My clothes…*

He strode into the bathroom to scoop them up then jogged downstairs and out into the back yard. Carl stared up at his neighbors' windows to check if any lights blazed. They didn't. Satisfied he was safe, he piled the clothes on the grass before going inside to get some lighter fluid and matches. Back out in the yard, he doused the clothes then set them on fire, watching the red, yellow and orange flames devour the fabric, thankful they burned despite being damp from the rain. Dark gray smoke billowed upward, gusting his way on a sudden stiff breeze. It caught at the back of his throat, and he coughed, returning inside for a glass of water and closing the back door so the smell didn't get in.

Carl stared through the window at the flames for long moments, replaying the killings and fabricating scenarios. *Would* the police call on him with regards to Paul? And if they did, what would he say? He shrugged.

I'll deal with that if it comes to it.

He went back outside, pleased to see the fire had gone out

and only ash and small material remnants remained.

What if the police call round and see this?

He clamped his jaw tight, thinking.

I'll vacuum it up tomorrow.

Pleased with his ingenious idea, he turned and headed back inside — inside to bed, where he could rest his weary body after a damn fine night's work.

Chapter Four

Much as I tried, sleep kept dancing back, just out of my reach. Every bone ached, and despite Lil's reassurances, I wasn't convinced ribs hadn't been cracked. He said bruised, but I figured that was quibbling. Like calling the Atlantic Ocean a pond. Semantics. Pain was pain, and it pushed sleep away just the same.

It didn't help that the couch, while comfortable, as far as it went, was way too close to their bedroom door. The thing wasn't soundproof. I knew Brian and Lil were trying to be quiet. I knew they needed the release sex gave. I'd seen the tension I'd brought into their home stretching Lil's shoulders tight and straight and pinching the skin around Brian's mouth into a glower. I'd noticed how close he'd stayed to Lil, and how free Lil had been with his reassuring caresses. In public, they weren't a demonstrative couple, so the dynamic surprised me. I'd always imagined Brian holding the fragile cross-dresser together, and now, well, maybe I'd had it backward all that time.

They quieted, eventually, and I found a relatively restful position half-sitting against the tall arm of the couch with my head propped on a thick cushion. I flung a heavy quilt around my shoulders then dozed. Flashes of the previous day and night kept pulling me back, shaking and sweating, into the dark, quiet living room. I ended up just staring into the blackness. Oddly, the thing that finally banished Carl's anger-distorted face and the memory of his violence from my mind was the thought of the stranger from the park. Just his face, the way he'd watched me as the car had passed. I was used to people leering like they wanted me.

Guys especially, who figured a pretty, skinny little thing would be an easy lay. And normally, before Carl had become possessive, they'd have been right. But that wasn't what I remembered seeing in that park guy's eyes. I didn't know what it was. Just not lust.

I didn't really notice that the dark had become less so until the bedroom door opened quietly. Lil emerged into the living room, followed closely by Brian, a sheet draped around his bare shoulders. He walked Lil to the front door and leaned on him as Lil wrapped his arms around him.

"You're going to be okay," Lil said.

Brian gazed up into his face, nodded then straightened.

"Good boy." Lil cupped Brian's face, kissed him firmly. "Don't leave him alone here, yeah?"

I almost surged up, livid he would think I couldn't be trusted, but his brow drew down, a grim mask taking over his features as he kept talking.

"He needs you with him. He might not be my favorite person, but he shouldn't be alone right now."

Brian nodded, and I sank back, confused.

"And remember what I said. Do not let that asshole in this apartment."

"I'm a big boy, Lil." Brian straightened a bit and squared his shoulders. "Carl does not scare me."

"He scares me. He'll want to get Paul back, one way or another. He'll start with flowers and candy, and I don't care if he sings a fucking love ballad. Do not let him in — do not leave Paul alone with him."

"You don't really think Paul would go back to Carl now?"

"I know people like Carl. I know how they work. They get under your skin."

He shivered and pulled Brian closer to him, seemingly more for his own comfort this time. Memories, maybe?

"Trust me, babe." He kissed the top of Brian's head. I'd never really noticed the height difference before. "Ice cream and old movies on the couch. Undivided attention that has nothing to do with Carl or sex. I said I would help you with

Paul, and I will. Do what I'm telling you. He needs this. I'll try and get home early if I can. And please don't go to the pool. Just stick close to home and be safe."

Brian maneuvered himself away from his lover again. "Life doesn't stop —"

"Paul's boyfriend raped him. Whatever either of them calls it, that's what happened. Some things can go into a bit of a holding pattern while he deals with that. Besides, you didn't see the bruises. I doubt he'll give you much argument if you suggest staying home and not showing that shit off to the world."

"Okay." Brian gave him one last kiss, held the door, and handed him his coat.

Lil slipped it on over his scrubs.

"Have a good shift," Brian said.

Lil smiled. "I'll be thinking of you, lover."

Brian stood in front of the closed door for a few minutes after Lil had left, and I wished I could see his face. I wasn't up to the chat that would happen if he knew I'd overheard their conversation, though, so I closed my eyes long before he turned toward me, and I kept them closed when he came over to the couch. I almost flinched as he stroked my hair, but long practice in holding back my reactions to Carl's touch kept me still.

"I am not letting you go back there," he whispered.

The blanket moved, pulled up and snugged around my shoulders, then he left. He went to his room and didn't come out until I shuffled past his half-open door an hour later, on my way to the bathroom.

* * * *

"Coffee?"

Brian stood by the kitchen window, facing outside as I returned to the living room and dressed.

"Sure," I said.

He didn't move. "You want to talk about it?"

"About coffee?" I pulled on an old pair of jeans then started doing up the buttons. "Cream and sugar. Baileys, if you've got it."

"We don't." He turned around, and the color drained from his cheeks a bit.

I supposed most of the really bad bruises hadn't developed when he'd seen me tied to the bed. They had now, layered over older marks. I'd just spent a good ten minutes examining my torso in the bathroom mirror. I knew what he was seeing. And what he wasn't.

'Paul's boyfriend raped him.'

I could practically hear the echo of Lil's statement in the air.

I wondered if Brian was going to ask me if that were true. I wondered what I'd tell him.

"I think I'll call the kids," was all he said. "Cancel swim practice."

I nodded. This wasn't something to try explaining to a bunch of teenage boys.

"We can run relays on Wednesday. Only takes one coach," he said.

"Life doesn't stop," I said quietly, not looking at him. I snagged a sweater then pulled it over my head. I didn't know if he picked up on the echo of his earlier conversation with Lil. When my head emerged from the collar, he was pouring cream into a cup of coffee.

We spent the next hour feeling around the emotional bruises as we talked almost in code, and trying to figure out where the whole mess left us. A lull in conversation stretched tight over something he wanted to ask, but I wasn't sure I wanted to answer, so I shuffled to the couch when he gathered the mugs and took them to the sink. I supposed it would be easier for him if I wasn't sitting across from him, watching the way his nerves clenched his fingers into fists he repeatedly had to flatten out onto the tabletop.

"I never would have left you alone with him, Paul. I didn't know he would…"

I waited. Seemed that was the end of the sentence, though. "Not your fault," I said at last. "He wasn't always like that, you know." I wanted to say he had been like Lil, when we'd started our relationship. Strong, in charge, good to me. But from what I'd seen the past day and a half, Carl was nothing like Lil. Brian wasn't afraid to ask for what he wanted. He'd asked Lil to help me, knowing Lil hated my guts, and he hadn't worried about reprisals. No. Carl was *definitely* nothing like Lil. I wanted what Brian had. Maybe that's what I'd been searching for. And why I'd hung on so long.

"Bri?" I twisted a bit to peer over the back of the couch at him. Brian turned around. "If he comes — "

As if on cue, someone knocked on the door. I knew the panic showed. How could it not? Though I was sitting, I felt like I might collapse, the blood drained so fast. Brian's face shifted to a grim expression.

"Go in the bedroom." He moved to the door but didn't open it. "Go!"

I stumbled up, unsure. I couldn't, shouldn't leave him alone with Carl. I remembered the way Carl had looked at me yesterday, pleased with the deliberate pain he'd caused when fucking me, as though he'd thought he might be abrading away any contact Brian might have had with me. I couldn't let him turn that anger on Brian.

The knock came again, a little louder, more insistent, and Brian bit his lip. "Paul, please."

I sidestepped around the corner, out of sight of the door, but didn't go too far. Brian peeked through the peephole. His shoulders released their tension almost immediately, and he yanked the door open.

"Vic!"

A tall, broad-shouldered man strode inside, and Brian shut the door behind him.

"Hey," the guest said. "Lil around?"

"He's at work." Brian smiled. "Come on in. I have coffee."

Vic pulled out a kitchen chair and sat. I couldn't take my

eyes off his face. This was the guy from the park. There was no way I could mistake those eyes, the perfect, high cheekbones, or dark glow of his skin.

"I guess you saw the news last night?" Vic took the steaming mug Brian offered and set it on the table.

"Yeah." Brian sat in the chair opposite him. "Anyone we know?"

Vic shook his head. "No. Never seen either of them before. The second one was married. Glad I didn't have to deliver that bad news. 'Ma'am, I'm sorry to have to tell you this, but we found your husband, pants open, throat slashed, body mutilated behind a gay bar!' Fuck. This is a mess."

"Two?"

Brian seemed to fold in on himself, and the motion drew me out of hiding to put a hand on his shoulder. He reached up and touched my fingers. The warmth of contact that didn't hurt was surprisingly reassuring.

"Vic," Brian said. "This is Paul Murdoch."

Vic turned his attention on me and his mouth fell open. Shocked recognition crossed his features, then, for one split second, he appeared horror-stricken. "Shit." His face went completely blank.

"Paul Murdoch." He stood, reached to his belt then pulled his badge free to hold it up in my face. "You are under arrest for the murder of Henry Staffville."

"What?" I stared, processing nothing at first, mesmerized by the glint of light dropping from the kitchen's pendant fixtures onto the stamped metal of the badge.

The words he'd spoken slammed into me, knocked my breath out, but they'd meant nothing right away. Not until he stepped behind me, grabbed one arm, and yanked it back did the meaning register. And then, my default to cowed submission was so ingrained he had me cuffed in a matter of seconds. I couldn't have resisted if I'd thought of it. Brian surged to his feet.

"Vic!"

"I'm sorry, Brian," Vic said.

I didn't know this Vic. Who knew if he really was sorry? But the professional veneer slipped as he returned to where I could see him, and met Brian's gaze.

"I have no choice." He turned to me and rattled off what I guessed were supposed to be my rights, but I didn't hear any of it.

"Bri?" I moved toward him. He could set this cop straight. This wasn't right.

"Victor, this is ridiculous! He didn't kill anyone!"

Brian inserted himself between the door and me, and I realized Victor had a hand on my back, shoving me in the direction of the exit. I stumbled and would have fallen on my face if Victor hadn't caught me by one arm. He hauled me upright, but his grip wasn't harsh. He met my eye, and I couldn't turn away.

"It's my job." His blank expression softened. "I didn't expect to see you here, Paul. I'm sorry. But there's a warrant. I can't ignore that."

"For murder? No." Brian planted his feet, crossed his arms. "No. I don't care about any warrant. He didn't do whatever it is you think he did."

"Who says *I* think it?" Victor's grip on my arm loosened a little more as he pursed his lips and drew his eyebrows together. "Everything about this case is cocked up. I'm on a short leash as it is, Bri, and if I'm going to figure any of it out, I have to go by the book. Please, please don't make me arrest you too."

"I'm telling you, he didn't do it," Brian said.

Victor studied him for a minute, then me, and a tic twitched his lips. There was that look in his eyes again. The one I couldn't interpret. I swallowed, trying to process what was going on.

"You must…" I had to clear my throat and still struggled to get my voice above a stunned whisper. "Have the wrong guy. I didn't…"

Victor gave himself a tiny shake, focused back on Brian. "Call Lil. Call a lawyer. Get out of my way."

"Please." This time, I didn't let him push me closer to the door. "Please, I didn't. I was here—"

"Don't." Victor moved his hand from my arm to my shoulder. "Let me do my job. It's the best way I can help you."

"You're arresting me!" I spat the words at him, feeling like a trapped, feral cat, hissing and ineffectual.

He tightened his fingers. "I have no choice. There's evidence we can't ignore, so come with me. You'll get a chance to explain yourself."

"You've already got me in restraints." I yanked on my hands, and the pain of the hard cuffs against tender wrists sharpened my focus. I remembered what Lil had said last night about them needing to find their cop killer. "You don't want an explanation. You want an arrest. You're desperate to pin this shit on anyone you can find. Who's going to listen?"

"I will. I have my own theories on what's going on, but I have to work within the rules, and the rules say I have to take you in."

"I'm no one to you, except a convenient fall guy. Who the hell would ever think I killed anyone? I've never even heard of Henry...whatever. What evidence do you have? Where did you get my name?"

He didn't respond. He stepped in front of me, lips pursed, but those dark eyes were earnest. "That isn't true—about you being a fall guy. Not to me. You don't know me, I know that, but I've been keeping close tabs on you recently. I'm not going to let anyone hurt you."

"Who the hell are you?" My voice wavered. I didn't realize I was shaking until he ran his hand down my bare arm and brushed my inner elbow with his thumb. The shaking turned to a shiver, and I gasped.

"You have to trust me," he said.

"I don't know you."

He glanced over to Brian, a slightly pleading look on his face. "Tell him."

"Tell him what? What do you want me to tell him? You're arresting him."

"I have to!"

"Why? You said evidence. What evidence?" Brian moved his fists to his hips.

"I can't tell you that."

I shifted to face Vic better, maybe to get that focus back on me. It shouldn't, but his gaze, his touch, calmed me. "Why have you been watching me?"

"Your boyfriend..." His eyes darkened, and the hand on my arm twitched. "I've come across him before. He's not a nice man."

"You think?"

He leaned closer. "If I could have talked you into leaving him, would you have?"

I swallowed a hefty dose of anger. He was right. Until yesterday, I wouldn't have listened to Brian and Lil, never mind a complete stranger.

"I know this is cocked up. This is not how I wanted things to go, but I'm here, you're here, and if it got out that I didn't take you in when I had the chance, I'd be done. I'm on thin ice as it is, and I need to keep myself in this investigation. It's the only way to get the *right* man. Please. I know it doesn't seem like it right now, but you can trust me. You have to. I'll prove you didn't do it."

"How?"

"I'll prove who did."

"You know who did?"

"Yes. I just have to get at him long enough to prove it. You might be able to help me do that."

"How?"

"Trust me."

"Just like that." I rattled the cuffs on my wrists. "How are you going to protect me when I'm in jail?"

That's when he turned back to Brian. "Get him a lawyer. Get down to the station. I'll delay as long as I can. Just be fast."

Brian nodded. He'd resigned himself to this, and there was nothing I could do. He wasn't backing me.

"I'll be right behind you, Paul."

I was shaking again. "This isn't right. You know I didn't do anything, Bri."

"I know. I'll get you a lawyer. I'll call Lil. We'll be there."

"I didn't…"

Brian stepped grimly aside, allowing Victor access to the door and letting him haul me out.

"Bri?"

Victor barely stopped long enough for me to get my feet into my shoes and for Brian to drape a jacket over my shoulders. He straightened it as I passed then patted my shoulder. "We'll be there. Promise."

"I didn't."

"I know."

I sighed, a loud huff of relief. I'd needed him to say it again. I had to hear it, even though I knew he believed me. "Thank you."

Outside, Vic's car sat right on the curb, and he opened the back door to maneuver me inside. I bent and folded into the seat, glanced up at him, and he actually smiled.

"I promise, I'll keep you safe. The charges are based on so little. It's going to be okay."

I nodded. Why was it so easy to believe him?

He closed the door, and I glanced at the front entrance of Brian's building. I half-expected to see Carl there grinning at me. He'd enjoy this. He'd be pissed when he didn't find me in my apartment. I just hoped to hell he didn't go looking for me at Brian's.

Chapter Five

Carl woke with a banging headache. Last night's activities had worn him out, what with the adrenaline rush, his anger toward Paul, and every goddamn grievance heaped upon him during his life pushing him to do what he'd done. He stared at the ceiling, thoughts of his childhood seeping into the edges of his brain. He hated looking back. After all, what was the point in harping on about regrets and things he couldn't change? Yet every so often, it was like his mind forced him to return to that shadowy place that still haunted him, a place he'd escaped from. Or so he'd thought.

Disliking the lack of control these memories gave him, he clenched his teeth to ward off the images, but they came regardless. *Shit.* He didn't need a dose of guilt right now. Didn't need to think about why he behaved as he did.

But the remembrance of those times as a kid butted at him, insistent that he listen to the voices of the past and watch the images flashing before him. His throat swelled with emotion and the knowledge of what he'd see and hear, and he closed his eyes, allowing those times to swamp him with their weighty oppression...

Moonlight's fingers clawed around little Carl's Superman bedroom curtains, and a low-watt lamp glowed on a chest of drawers at the bottom of his bed. He didn't like night-times. Didn't like what they brought.

"You're a damn jerk of a kid sometimes, Carl," his father said, leering grin too close, eyes round and bloodshot. "Got no idea where you get your bad behavior from, 'cause it sure ain't from me." His breath fanned Carl's face. Rancid. Evil. "Reckon your

bitch of a mother's to blame. Fucking off and leaving us."

Carl shrank back in his bed, nine-year-old eyes wide, the covers clutched beneath his chin. His father, the son of a bitch named Kevin, sat on the edge, in baggy sweatpants. A filthy white vest gaped at the neck. Kevin pulled away and stared at the wall, elbows on knees, dangling his hands between them. Carl wondered what his father saw when he gazed like that, all bug-eyed and slack-jawed. Carl squinted, taking in Kevin's stubbled, ruddy cheeks and big stout nose. A shudder snaked up his spine, and he drew the blankets farther up so only his eyes and the top of his head showed.

"So, you got in trouble at school again, fuck-wit, huh?" Kevin kept staring ahead and rasped his palm over his chin.

The noise shrieked in the quiet room, and Carl blinked, hot tears pricking his eyes.

"No point in answering me, 'cause that fat bitch from the school called. Told me all about it. Getting in fights, huh? Been going on for some time, she said. Carl's a bad influence, she said. Carl's a bad boy, she said." He sighed. "And you know what happens to bad boys, right?"

Carl's stomach churned. Oh, he knew what happened all right. Any minute now, Kevin would pick up that belt he'd dropped to the floor when he'd come into the room and lift it high into the air, bringing it down, down, down…

Carl needed to pee. He willed himself not to, but the hot trickle of urine burned his thighs and seeped between them, onto the mattress beneath his ass. When Kevin whipped the covers back, he'd see. He'd know. And that belt…sure as shit it'd hit him harder.

I can't help being bad. I'm sorry. I don't mean to, I just… I want Mom. I want her back here so she can hug it all away, make Dad stop…

Kevin stood, fists bunched, and paced beside the bed. "D'you know, kid, that when you love someone, you are all they need. You diggin' me?" He stopped walking and glared down at Carl.

Nervous as hell, Carl shook from head to foot, unable to control his body. The piss had cooled, itched his legs, but he couldn't *bring himself to let go of the covers to scratch them.*

He'll start on me in a minute, just like he always does.

Kevin's brow furrowed, and his dark eyes darkened some more, as though the irises had bled into the brown. "I see you don't get what I'm saying. Take you and me, as an example. I love you, right, and everything I do is because I love you. I show you that love with discipline." He resumed pacing and shook his head. "I tell you, you'll understand when you're older, when you love someone and they rip your fucking heart out. So, when you do find that person you love over anyone else, you gotta keep them in line, make them understand your love with authority. It's the only way, kid. And another thing" — he reached down for the belt — "when you get that special person in your life, you've gotta take away every danger, every other person that threatens your relationship, 'cause if you don't, they'll fuck you over and screw with you. Leave you broken. D'you get that?"

Carl nodded, quick sharp bobs of the head that hurt his neck.

"So never forget what I just said, right? And now you understand why I gotta do what I'm gonna." Kevin wrenched the covers back, widening his eyes, his mouth gaping at Carl's midsection. "You gone and pissed again, kid?"

A sob left Carl, and snot shot out of his nose onto his top lip. With his balled hands over his mouth, he bit a knuckle and closed his eyes tight.

"Lift your damn arms," Kevin said.

Carl obeyed.

It's coming, it's coming, it's coming…

The sound of the belt whizzing through the air reached him a millisecond before the leather cracked across his chest. The burn killed, and he instinctively raised his knees to his chest.

"Knees down, kid."

The belt slapped again and again, until Carl peed once more and sobbed, his knuckles bleeding from his bite. After the last strike, tears streaming down his face, Carl opened his eyes. Kevin was gone, but the filthy stench of him remained — his sour breath, his fetid body odor. Carl blew out through shaky lips and, wincing, got out of bed. His chest ached, throbbed, and as he walked to the closet, fresh tears spilled. He opened the door then gingerly bent down to take a clean sheet off the wardrobe floor. Once he'd stripped his bed, he went out onto the landing and dumped the wet sheets in the laundry hamper then collected a towel from the airing cupboard. Back in his room, he laid the folded towel over the piss and remade the bed, every movement agony.

He kneeled beside his bed and clasped his hands together, closing his eyes.

"Please, God, let me be just like my daddy. If I'm not, he'll hurt me some more."

Carl fisted the tears away, angry that his past still had the ability to affect him this way. He should be over it by now, god-fucking-damn-it! He got out of bed then stomped into the bathroom. He set the shower to hot.

The hotter the better. Burn those bastard memories away.

He stepped inside the cubicle, bracing himself for yet another reminder of the past as the hot spikes of water seared his torso. He thought of Paul, how his chest must have burned last night, how he would have pissed the bed just like Carl used to do if Paul hadn't gotten free. Tears mingled with the water splashing on his face, and he swallowed past the lump in his throat.

'When you get that special person in your life, you've gotta take away every danger, every other person that threatens your relationship, 'cause if you don't, they'll fuck you over and screw with you. Leave you broken…'

He ground his teeth and grabbed the shower gel, washing away the grime of his childhood, the way the memories made him feel. He stared as the lather disappeared into the plughole, wishing every horrible thing he'd endured went down there right along with it. He closed his eyes, and Paul's face danced on the insides of his eyelids.

I can't be without him. He's got to see how much I love him. He took in a deep breath and forced all the shit away, concentrating on what he had to do next. *I've removed six threats, six men that could have possibly taken Paul from me, but there's one son of a bitch who poses a greater threat than anyone.*

He shut the shower off then toweled himself dry as he walked into his bedroom to dress. Once clothed, he sat on the bed and pulled on his boots, then strutted downstairs to the hallway to shrug into his coat. Pausing at the door, he contemplated the scenario of whether the police had found the credit card he'd dropped. Had the last two murders made the news? The ones before hadn't, and he'd been angry about that. If they made the news, Paul would see how much Carl cared, what lengths he went to, to show his love.

It would only take a moment to check. He rushed into the living room and turned on the TV, flicking to the news channel. A presenter waffled about the economy and the state of the country's finances, and he jabbed a button on the remote to change to another channel. Once again, the anchor gassed on, but Carl wasn't listening. He was too busy reading the words streaming from right to left across the bottom of the screen, white words on a red-banded background.

He smiled, punched the air then switched off the TV, elation surging through him that his love for Paul had been spelled out on screen for all to see. A man had been arrested, hopefully Paul.

A wave of determination propelled him back to the front door, and he swung it wide, snatching his car keys from the side table next to it. Outside, he climbed into the driver's seat then gunned the engine, ready to eradicate one more motherfucker from their lives.

The drive there proved pleasant, with little traffic, which gave him time to think over exactly what he was going to do. Yes, his actions would prove Paul wasn't the killer they were after, but when Paul got released, he'd run to Carl for comfort. Yes, Carl had it all worked out.

He slowed to a stop at a set of lights and drummed the steering wheel with his fingertips while he waited for them to change.

Man, you're gonna wish you'd never met me, and when you see my bad side, after I've explained why you're the next one on my list, you'll understand why I gotta do what I'm gonna.

Maniacal laughter erupted from him at the realization that he'd thought some of his father's words, and he threw his head back, setting the hilarity free. He composed himself quickly and glanced inside a car that pulled up beside his. The woman driver gave him a frightened stare, and Carl laughed again, power infusing his bones, his muscles, his whole goddamn body. He whipped his head around to face forward, saw the lights had switched, and sped off toward his destination.

Outside the apartment block, he eyed the place and parked between two other cars hogging the roadside. Before getting out, he looked around, conscious that he played a dangerous game here. Too many people could see him if they stared out of their windows, but he didn't have a choice. He had to do this. Had to see it through. Sighing, he got out of the car. Locked it, keeping his head down as he made his way into the apartment block. Taking the stairs two at a time, he reached the door he needed and pressed an ear to it. The tinny sound of a TV at low volume filtered out, as well as the shuffle of feet belonging to a lethargic person.

Yeah, he's lethargic all right. Big old bastard's tired from screwing that drip of a dick he calls his boyfriend.

The man's height and size gave him reason to pause. Could he do what he had to do? Could he overpower the big guy quickly enough to slit his thick throat?

Fuck yeah!

Carl raised his fist then rapped on the door, the action paining his knuckles.

The door opened, and Brian stood on the other side.

"What do *you* want?" Brian said, his wide frame almost filling the space between each jamb. His scowl showed his displeasure at seeing Carl, and his mouth formed a thin, tight line.

Carl held back laughter. "Mind if I come in?" He barged past Brian before he had a chance to protest and stalked into the living room. The door slamming irked him, and he spun to face the big man as he entered the room. The thrill of what he had planned sped through him, and he smirked at Brian's thunderous expression. *Fucking jerk.* "No *girl*friend around?"

Brian narrowed his eyes. "If you mean *Lil*, then no. He's at work. What the fuck do you want, Carl? Say what you have to say and get out."

"That's not very charitable behavior, now, is it?" Carl shoved his hands in his pockets, curling the fingers of one around his flick knife.

"You don't deserve charitable behavior. Not after what you did to Paul." Brian crossed his arms over his chest and planted his feet wide apart.

Bully-boy pose. What a prick.

"And what did I do to Paul, exactly?" The knife warmed from his skin's heat. He'd have to bring it out soon or risk losing his grip from the sweat forming on his palms.

"Don't piss me about, Carl. You know what you did to him. I'll ask you once more. What do you want?"

Carl smiled and strolled out of the living room and back into the hallway. He faced Brian, who turned and stepped forward, leaning on the doorjamb. Swiftly, Carl brought his hand out of his pocket and flicked the blade free, lunging toward Brian with such speed, the blade pressed to the big brute's neck before he had a chance to react. The point jabbed into his skin, and Brian raised both hands, eyes wide and wary, cheeks flushing red.

"Whoa! Calm it, will you?" Brian said, darting his eyes left then right and finally focusing solely on Carl.

Adrenaline whooshed through Carl, and he savored the lightheaded sensation, the feeling almost like a drug. The sweat of power broke out over his back and forehead, and he pressed the blade harder, the point breaking the skin. Blood trickled, a meandering path that glossed over Brian's

Adam's apple and into the hollow beneath.

"Calm it? *Calm* it?" Carl itched to flick the knife to the right and watch the bastard drop to the floor. "You've been nothing but a fucking thorn in my side ever since I met Paul. Poking your damn nose in, giving unwanted advice. Do *you* want some advice?"

Brian didn't answer. He widened his eyes further as the blade dug deeper, and his hands shook.

"*Do you?*" Carl shouted, pulse thudding in his ears.

Brian nodded slightly, lower lip trembling, and his eyes watered.

"Don't fuck with me and mine. I don't like it. Don't tolerate it. Won't put up with it." Carl moved one step closer, blade hand steady, the other gripping the jamb to give him the brace needed when he drew the knife across.

"It was you, wasn't it?" Brian asked, voice steady and low.

"Me what?" Carl clenched his teeth, hatred for Brian snatching his breath and infusing him with strength.

"You who...who killed those men." Brian's eyes closed momentarily. He swallowed, and his Adam's apple bobbed.

Carl jerked the knife, and a fresh drizzle of blood seeped down Brian's neck.

"Damn fucking right it was me." Carl glared at him, memories of every time the man had butted in leaching into his mind. Ire boiled, bubbled over, and he gripped the knife handle, ready to—

The sound of a key sliding into the front door lock sounded, and Brian darted his eyes in that direction. Carl moved to slash, but Brian lowered his hands then brought one up beneath Carl's arm, jerking it upward and away. Brian reared up a bit and pushed Carl's chest. Incensed beyond measure, Carl sprawled backward, thumping against the hallway wall as the front door opened, shielding him from view.

"Behind the door! Lil! Be careful!" Brian yelled. "He's got a knife!"

"What?" said Lil. "I come home early, and you — "

"Lil!" Brian shouted.

Lil strode into the living room, and Carl stepped out from behind the door, charging forward, knife raised, poised to plunge it into Lil's back.

"Lil!" Brian leaped forward, shoving Lil out of the way, putting himself between Carl and Lil.

Mistake.

Carl grinned, lunged, and felt the satisfying sensation of steel sliding into flesh. He pulled back and stabbed again, this time meeting resistance almost immediately.

Brian lurched away with a howl.

Landing on his side, head almost hitting the coffee table edge, Lil turned to face Carl, eyes wide and face blanched of all color. "You fucking..." He scrambled up, reaching for the phone on the coffee table.

Brian approached, and Carl reversed out of the front doorway.

He was supposed to stay down!

The knife was slick with blood now, too hard to grip.

"Fucker," Carl said, turning quickly then running for the main block stairwell.

Hard footsteps followed him, and he sped down the stairs, almost tripping, the squeak of his shoe soles loud in the confined space. At the bottom, he burst outside, racing toward his car. Clicking his key fob to unlock it, he dove inside, hands shaking as he inserted the key into the ignition. He slammed the door closed and revved the engine, glancing to the side to see Brian thundering toward him. He cursed parking in such a tight spot, and his foot slipped on the accelerator. The car shunted forward, smacking into the rear bumper of the car in front. He reversed, pranging the car behind, and stared at Brian, who slapped the driver's-side window with his palms, his face red and eyes blazing, leaving behind a smeared, bloody handprint.

Attention back on maneuvering his car out, Carl ignored his fast-thudding heart and pulled out, heedless of a car coming his way. He floored the gas pedal and slewed across the road, narrowly missing the other moving vehicle. Fear and excitement pumping through him, he swerved out of the street then around the corner, the realization that he couldn't return home slamming into him.

That bitch Lil will have called the police. Shit.

Out on the main road, he took deep breaths to calm his speeding heart and soothe his stretched nerves. He spied a woman getting out of her car outside a large residence and failing to lock it as she carried paper grocery sacks to her front door. Carl brought his car to a stop a few feet away then shut off the engine. The woman went inside her house, and Carl exited his car, running to the woman's. He slid inside and thanked his lucky stars that keys swung in the ignition. Quickly, he started the car then drove away slowly so as not to alert the owner with screeching tires. As he prepared to turn the corner at the end of her street, he glanced in the rear-view mirror. The woman stood on the sidewalk where her car had been parked, hands on hips, a look of confusion on her face.

Carl turned right and laughed his adrenaline-fueled ass off.

Chapter Six

Vic, I mean the cop — why I thought we were on a first-name basis eluded me at the moment — didn't speak as he'd maneuvered the car away from Brian's building. His facial expression was grim then blank — except his eyes. They were too deep, too intent. That look sent shivers through me, like he was trying to memorize my face, trying to see into my head, trying to...

"What?" My question came out harsh. Yeah. It had sounded surly. Fear did that to a person.

I shifted, trying to ease the ache of shoulders held at an awkward, humiliating angle by the cuffs. The metal bit right through the bandages Lil had applied, and the pain cleared away some of the fog of shock. "You keep staring. What's your problem?"

"What do you see in him?"

"Brian?" What the hell was going through his head? "He's my best friend. We've been —"

"No. Not Brian. I know that. I know how long you've known him. I know..." He wove through traffic, chewed on his lip, glanced at my reflection, and seemed to come to some decision that eased a bit of the tension out of his grip on the wheel. "I know about you. Your mother died when you were twelve, your father turned mean. Brian protected you. You both swam on the varsity team in high school and won a lot. You went to college with him, and now you coach an inner-city kids' swim team. You have one kid on the team who could be Olympic standard if he can get funding. Two years ago, you started culinary school but dropped out when Carl came along, and what the fuck do you see in that jackass?"

I blinked. "You a cop or a stalker?"

He sighed, and his focus drifted back to the road and the red light he'd stopped at. For a few minutes, he didn't say anything. His hands on the wheel, ten and two, were stiff again, like holding it kept him grounded.

"Too fucking close," he muttered.

"What?" I leaned forward, shifting to find a clear view through the mesh separating us.

He tightened his lips into a pinched line. The light turned green. Seconds ticked by. A horn sounded impatiently, and he jerked, a miniscule quiver of his entire body. The car rolled forward, and he loosened his fingers. He glanced over his shoulder, searching out my face, rather than settling for my reflection in the rear-view mirror. "People want to protect you," was all he said before swiveling back around and concentrating on the road again.

My spine began to ache with the strain of leaning forward. I sank back into the seat and glared out of the window. "Carl used to say that. Never knew what he thought I needed protecting from."

Maybe himself.

"Maybe himself?" Vic voiced my thought.

My heart flipped over, and I shot a look into the mirror. Vic was watching me again.

"He's a dangerous man, Paul."

"You think?"

Vic drew in a deep breath. There was something loitering just under the surface. Something he wasn't saying. Something he wanted to say, but wouldn't let himself, I guessed.

"Do you know anything about his past?"

I shook my head. I'd told Carl a few things about my dad once, and he'd shut me up about it. "We didn't talk about our childhoods. He didn't..."

I shivered. Saying 'didn't like to' was an understatement. He'd about gone ballistic when I'd told him some of the out-of-control things my father had done when he drank.

"He had an ugly childhood," Vic stated.

"Huh." I'd figured that much out on my own. After that first violently aborted conversation, I hadn't asked for details. That wasn't the kind of thing a person like Carl relived with impunity, and his pain never translated to something I could bear much of.

"Do you love him?"

Vic's question caught me off guard. His voice had changed — gone from cop to something else.

"What the fuck business is that of yours?" I should have been more angry, felt more violated he'd ask something like that. I was sitting in cuffs, on my way to who the hell knew what, and we were talking about goddamn fucking Carl. That indignation eclipsed a bit of my fear.

"It isn't any of my business," he admitted.

Yet he met my eye in the mirror, and I had the feeling he was still waiting for an answer. And I didn't have one. Carl had beaten me and, I had to admit, Lil was right. For all I hadn't resisted Carl, I hadn't wanted that last round. It hadn't been sex, just a form of violence that hurt less than fists or his belt. And he'd left me helpless and in danger. How could I love a man who did that?

I broke the eye contact first. "He didn't start out that way…"

"They never do."

"Guess you hear this shit a lot, huh?"

Vic snorted. "You think hearing it over and over makes it any easier to listen to?"

"Probably just makes you wonder what all the saps are thinking, getting caught in it. You'd have to be an idiot to let it go that far."

"No one thinks you're an idiot, Paul."

I chewed on the inside of my lip and said nothing.

"Brian and Lil are just worried sick."

It all clicked into place. Of course. He knew Brian. He would know all about me.

"Brian's a good guy," I said. "I doubt Lil worries about me any more than beyond my bad influence on his lover." I had to give Lil credit, though. He was a lot more charitable about Brian's concern for me than I was about putting up with him.

A chuckle from the front seat startled me into drawing my gaze from the guardrail posts flinging past outside and back to the mirror.

"You have no idea. Lil's been through shit. He knows bad times. He'd do for you even if Brian didn't ask, because he's been there." Vic's deep brown eyes met mine again. "Brian and Lil's brother, they had a lot in common." He left the explanation dangling a moment as he pulled into the police station and around back, then shut off the engine. "They lost Lil for a long time, inside himself, when he was figuring his shit out. But he did figure it out, and Jason was so hopeful, so ready to get his brother back, you know? They both wanted that so much it hurt to watch.

"Nothing hurts worse than making those mistakes, losing everything, and just when you think you're going to get back what's most important, having it torn away like what happened to Lil. He wouldn't sit back and watch it happen to someone else."

I nodded, understanding. Lil would do for me what he had to in order to protect Brian, to keep him from the pain of losing a brother, because essentially, blood or not, that's what we were to each other.

"I have to take you in now."

Just like that, the fear slammed back into my gut, and I felt the blood drain from my face. "Please don't do this." Every nightmare Carl had visited on me screamed along my nerves at the thought of being surrounded by a dozen like him. "I don't know how... I didn't... I was at Brian's all night. On his couch. I—"

Vic pursed his lips, got out of the car then came round to open my door.

I didn't move.

"Paul." He said my name so softly.

It almost sounded reassuring, and I forced my gaze up to him, squinting at the morning sun grinding into my eyes over his shoulder.

He glanced around as though making sure no one was watching, then he crouched down. "Will you trust me?"

I had a hard time keeping the dizzying panic away. I just stared at him.

"I am not going to let anything happen to you," he said.

"Why would you even care? You don't know me."

He smiled, a self-deprecating expression, and dropped his gaze for a fraction of a second. "I'm in over my head here, Paul. I know you didn't do anything. I know it like I know my own name. I would and I will stake my reputation as a good cop on it, but I cannot ignore the law. If I do, I lose all the power I have to help you."

"No one in there is going to believe me. You said they have evidence, and they want *someone*. Who will really care I'm the wrong one?"

Vic bit his lip, his face going grim enough to be an answer without his next words. "No. They want a perp. At this point, it doesn't matter who. Jason was a good cop, a good man, and he's been dead months. Having no leads is making them desperate and furious. They figure they've got their first break and they'll be hard to convince it isn't the right one."

"You were his partner. Why do you believe me?"

Again, that quirk of a smile, directed at some shortcoming of his own I wasn't seeing, crossed his face. "Because I... fell."

"Fell?"

He shook his head. "The night after Jason died, I went back to The Anchor. Don't even know why. To try and find what we missed, maybe. It was my first mistake. I was supposed to stay away, stay out of the investigation."

"He was your partner."

"Which is why I should have stayed away." He lifted his

gaze, and this time, there was no mistaking that he was not talking to me as a cop now.

I could have tumbled into those eyes, cuffs and all, and never come out.

"I saw you there, Paul. With Carl. I don't know what it was. Something he said, some way he hovered over you, or how you acted toward him. Something. I don't know, but it got my hackles up. When you went to the bathroom at one point, he slipped out the back door, and I followed him. He was standing in the alley, just inside the crime tape, staring at the spot we found Jason's body. He had the strangest look on his face. I can't even describe it, except I would not want to know what was going through his head at that moment. He went back inside, grabbed you and dragged you out. Like he was terrified."

Halfway through his story, I'd begun to shake. I remembered that night. I hadn't heard about Lil's brother yet, but I remembered Carl's sudden shift, from overbearing and protective to—something else.

He hadn't been afraid of anything. Not that I could tell. He'd been so horny he couldn't wait to get back to his place before getting his cock into me for the first round. He'd started in the car, and the entire night had been wild, forceful, and pushed just to edge of scary. An edge that had blurred and disintegrated before long and had ended with me tied to my own bed.

"He did it." The accusation fell off my lips, unstoppable. Horrifying. But undeniable.

"But I can't prove it." Vic's shoulders sagged. "In my gut I know it, but I can't prove a damn thing."

"How many?"

Vic dropped his head into his hand. "Paul—"

"How many!"

"Six. As far as I can tell."

"I need to—"

He raised his head, finally, and I found I couldn't meet his eye. "I'm sorry. I didn't do this right."

"I—" My gut churned. "Get me out of here." I struggled to get my feet free of the car and shirked past him.

He was up and grabbing for me in two strides, and too fucking bad I puked all over his shoes. If he'd thought I'd been about to run, it served him right. Where the hell was I going to go? It left me shaking and helpless to even wipe my mouth.

"Here." Vic lifted my chin, used the tail of his shirt to wipe the corner of my lips.

"Don't." I pulled away, tilting my head from his touch.

"I'm sorry. Paul, I dropped that on you—"

"Like a ton of bricks." I couldn't stop shaking.

"This whole thing is fucked up." He slid his hand from my chin to my shoulder where it rested, a warm, solid mass that I shouldn't have been taking comfort in. "You shouldn't be here. Not like this."

For one, delirious moment, I was sure he was going to reach around and release me. His hand grazed from my shoulder down my arm and stopped just above the cuffs.

"I should get you in there."

I might have actually whimpered. I couldn't make my feet move, though, and the slight tug Vic initiated on my arm eased.

"You don't have any reason to trust me," he said.

I kept my head down and my mouth shut.

"But I'll walk you through every step. I promise. You just tell the truth, and nothing bad can happen."

Something else Carl said a lot, only the bruises proved otherwise.

Vic's fingers twitched on my wrist then he trailed them up my arm. His body heat intensified as he stepped closer. "I believe you, Paul. I'm going to keep you safe. I'm going to get you out of this."

I clenched my teeth for a second. "You're the one getting me into it. Just let me go."

"And what will you do? Disappear? If you do, it will only look worse."

"Please." I risked raising my head, looking into his eyes, and braced for the impact of his intense focus. "Just let me go?"

He didn't do what I expected. He pulled me to him, snuck the hand on my arm around to the small of my back. I was pressed to his side, cheek flat against his broad chest, his breath wafting across my hair.

"The best way to keep you safe right now is to keep you where he can't get at you, where I can stay close, and we can prove you're innocent."

"Why?" Too many questions swirled through my head for me to get any of them out properly.

"I'll explain it all, I promise." He stepped away, and a chill breeze brought goosebumps up on my arms. "Right now, before anyone wonders what's going on, I have to take you inside. You'll have to answer questions. Lots of them. Over and over. Just tell the truth. I won't be far. I know it seems contradictory, but the only way I can help you is to protect my job."

"And Carl?"

"He can't hurt you now."

I smiled wryly at that. "He always finds a way."

Chapter Seven

Carl had abandoned the woman's car and was now inside the café of a service station, watching a man he'd seen park up outside earlier. The driver of a battered blue pickup truck sat scoffing down bacon, eggs and hash browns. Music blared from hidden speakers somewhere or other in the room, the sound tinny and thin. Carl spied a set of keys beside the man's plate and faked tripping, banging his hip into the table. Pain throbbed, and he cursed, apologizing to the greasy-haired fucker for disturbing him.

"Jesus, sorry about that, pal." Carl laid his hands on the tabletop, one curved over the keys. "Damn near sent your food flying."

The man stared at him, cheeks ruddy, nostrils flared in anger. He reminded Carl of his father, and Carl bit down the urge to uppercut the bastard's nose so the bone jabbed into his brain.

"You'd better watch what you're doing in future, *pal*," the man grumbled, shaking his head and turning back to his meal.

"Like I said, sorry." Carl coughed and swiped the keys at the same time, clutching them in his fist so they didn't jingle. He strode away from the table then out of the door, eyeing the vehicles parked in straight lines. He slipped the key into the pickup's lock, scoping the area then peering toward the café. Carl huffed out a laugh and climbed inside the truck. Damn fool man hadn't parked right outside the joint anyway, and this shit-hole of a place had no security cameras. Carl drove over to the woman's car he'd abandoned, grabbed the grocery sacks then transferred them to the pickup. With a full tank of gas, he hightailed it out of there, adrenaline spiking at what he'd done and what he was about to do.

He gritted his teeth, mind going over the next few hours. He'd reach the town of Hidcup in about fifty-five minutes. Someone he needed to see lived there, though the motherfucker wouldn't live there for much longer. No, Carl had anger boiling through him, pervading his whole goddamn body to the point he lost his breath. He inhaled deeply then released the air, telling himself to calm the hell down. If he wanted closure, if he wanted some semblance of a normal life, he had to see this through to its conclusion.

The deserted road stretched ahead, fields spread out either side, and Carl jabbed at the radio button to switch it on. Country music filtered out of the speakers, and he smiled wryly. *Figures. Matches that hick guy in the café.* He fiddled with the tuning dial until he found a classical station. The music soothed his rattled nerves, infusing him with the strength he needed. Serenity stole over him, bleeding into every part of his body, and his shoulders relaxed.

He drove the remainder of the journey in contemplation of the past. Scenes that usually disturbed him flickered through his head, but he watched them with detachment, as though he didn't star in every scenario. The kitchen of his youth came into view, and he knew then what he'd see.

"Say what?" his father said, eyes wide, mouth agape. He planted meaty hands on his hips, his paunch hanging over his jeans waistband, poking out from beneath his too-small vest like a pouch of bread dough.

"I said I'm leaving." Carl bunched his fists — fists the same size as his father's, his shoulders just as broad. "No reason to stay around here now." He picked up his holdall then slung it over his shoulder.

Kevin narrowed his eyes, and red splotches spread from small to large on his cheeks. "You tellin' me you don't need me now? Is that it? Like, I've brought you up on my own, and now you're eighteen you're just gonna fuck off?" He harrumphed, and spittle gathered at the corners of his mouth. "Well, that's just damn ungrateful, kid. I mean, is that all the thanks I get?"

Carl fought the frown itching to line his brow. *Is he for real?* "Am I meant to thank you for belting my ass, is that it? D'you want thanks for bringing me up? Is that what it'll take to make you happy?"

Kevin scrubbed his palm over his chin and paced the floor, his lengths limited, what with the narrow floor space between a wall of cabinets and the sink unit. "You need to watch your mouth."

"Watch my mouth? Didn't you ever think forward to this day? Did you really reckon I'd stick around?" Carl took his car keys off the hook on the wall then stuffed them in his pocket.

"You needn't think you're taking that fuckin' car!" Kevin lunged forward, hand outstretched for the keys.

"And you needn't think I'm not." Carl shoved him backward. "You don't give gifts then take them away. Fuck off, old man." He left the kitchen, left his father standing there bunching and unbunching his fists, arm muscles flexing along with his jaw. Outside, he tossed his holdall in the back of his car and slid into the driver's seat.

"Hey, you! Fuckin' wait a goddamn minute!" Kevin ambled out of the house, feet planted a foot apart on the slatted wooden porch, his arms curved at his sides as though he was ready to fight. He stepped off the porch and into the yard, heading for the car. "If you've gotta go, just you remember what I taught you, you hear me?"

"What's that, then?" Carl asked, knowing full well what he'd meant. He slammed the door closed then wound down the window.

"About keeping those you love in line. Teaching them how it goes. How it's gotta be."

Carl laughed and shook his head. "Like I could ever forget." He paused. "From what you told me, it applies to every relationship, right?"

Kevin beamed, his dirty teeth peeking from between wet lips. "You're goddamn right it does!"

Carl slid the key in the ignition and started the car. He raised his voice. *"So you won't mind me coming back in a few years and applying it to you, right?"* He gripped the steering wheel, palms sweating, heartbeat racing at the thought of his return.

"I'd like to see you try!" Kevin's hearty laughter burst out of him, his dough belly juddering.

Bile burned the back of Carl's tongue, and he swallowed it down. *"You would?"* He winked. *"That's good, then, because I'll be coming back for you."*

Kevin blinked, and his mouth worked with no sound coming out. He moved closer to the car, fist poised to strike through the open window. *"You what? You what?"*

"You heard me, old man. Now fuck off inside and enjoy the time you've got left."

Carl reversed down the short driveway at speed, missing the gatepost by a whisper. Out on the road, he smiled. It turned into laughter — that of someone who had found freedom from a lifetime of constraints, rules, and abuse — and drove with no destination in mind, uncaring where he ended up. Anywhere was better than back there.

WELCOME TO HIDCUP! The weathered wooden sign had Carl's stomach rolling. The familiar landscape on the outskirts, all scrubland and old-fashioned houses dating back to the 1920s, brought on a rush of memories, nostalgia for the happy times from his youth. There weren't many, he'd admit that, but summers spent climbing trees and playing war with his school buddies induced a sad smile. Only home held bad memories, and there were stacks of those for him to count. He grimaced and cleared his mind, turning down a right-hand road that led to his childhood home.

A wave of sadness enveloped him at the sight of the two-story situated halfway down the street. It looked the same, as though time had stopped and he'd only left yesterday. He parked up on the opposite side of the road then killed the engine, chuckling at the irony, for wasn't that what he'd come here to do? Kill the engine, the one thing that had kept him going since he'd been away? Hell yeah, he'd returned to take his life back, to douse out the life of the one person who prevented him moving on.

Carl rubbed his sweaty palms up and down his thighs then leaned into the back seat for a grocery bag. Hunger gripped his stomach, and he dumped the sack on his lap to rifle through the contents. He pulled out a package of sliced cheese and ripped it open before ramming two pieces into his mouth. It tasted good, so he finished the lot then dug into the bag again, bringing out a deli pack of salami. After eating it all, he rested his head back and stared at his old home through half-lidded eyes. His old man would be at work, if his past habits were anything to go by.

Getting out of the truck, Carl then locked it up. He strode across the road then walked up the driveway and onto the porch, his guts clenching and his heart ticking way too fast for his liking. It seemed as though he'd been transported back to his younger days, when coming home meant fear and admonishment. And the belt.

Breathing deeply, he took a set of keys out of his pocket, surprised to find his father hadn't changed the locks in all this time. He obviously hadn't taken Carl's threat seriously. Anger at Kevin's lack of belief burned in Carl's gut, and he stepped inside. Stale air smacked into him, the same aroma he'd smelled as a kid, the same dusty, moldy stench he'd vowed would never seep into his own home. He bit back a retch and closed the door. As he stood in the hallway, he felt like an intruder, yet at the same time, it was like he belonged. The walls held memories, which bled out now, taking him to places he didn't want to go. His eyes stung and he angrily swiped away the tears.

No. He's not going to affect me like this. Fucking jerk.

He prowled the house, noting everything remained the same. The kitchen still bore evidence of neglect, of a man who didn't know how to keep house. Teabags, dried and yellowed, sat in a pile on the countertop. Sugar grains from an obvious spill hadn't been wiped up. Dirty dishes stood piled in the sink, and the tap dripped, just like it always had, a steady plop-plip-plop, although those droplets seemed fatter now.

A damn washer change, that's all it'd take. Jesus.

Carl shook his head and turned from the squalor, making his way through the living room. Newspapers in a haphazard pile looked on the verge of slewing off the coffee table, down onto a floor in sore need of vacuuming. Dirt, food particles, and dust bunnies covered the beige carpet. The sofa sagged in the middle — the old spring that used to jab Carl's ass was a little more exposed now. A thick layer of dust covered the wooden sideboard, a circle of less-thick dust showing something had been recently moved. A cup, maybe.

Nothing's changed. Not a goddamn thing.

Upstairs, he pushed open his bedroom door, steeling himself for what he'd see.

Jesus Christ!

His bed remained exactly as he'd left it, the quilt bunched into a ball, the sheet and pillow bearing the shape of his body and head. A musky scent lingered, one of filth and corruption, of a kid growing up with no mother to clean the house or stroke a fevered brow. He swallowed the lump in his throat and blinked several times, determined to remain focused. His mind had other ideas, though. Where was his mother now? Did she ever think of the little boy she'd abandoned to a life of depravity and unhappiness? Had she moved on to a new relationship, with kids she'd baked cookies with and ensured were clean and well-fed? If she had, how did he feel about that? He didn't know, didn't want to entertain the thought of discovering half-siblings that reveled in the care he'd missed out on. It wasn't their fault, but shit, they were lucky bastards.

A phlegm-filled cough sounded, as though out in the back yard, and Carl moved to the window. He gazed down on the sandy, grotty area, at the old beige hammock he used to swing on with his eyes closed, the summer breeze tickling his tear-stained face. At Kevin, who now swung on that seat, hand-rolled cigarette between two fingers, smoke oozing out of his mouth.

What the fuck is he doing out there in this weather?

Though the sun shone, it was hardly warm enough to be outside, especially not in jogging bottoms and his customary stained vest. Carl studied his father. Not everything had remained the same, then. The old man had aged, his stubble tinted with gray, his hair peppered with it at the temples. He looked haggard and weak, and Carl smiled, pleased at the bastard's decline.

Taking in a deep breath, Carl left his bedroom to walk downstairs to the kitchen, standing at the closed back door. He regarded Kevin again through the dirty square of glass, the wrinkles on the old man's face evident at this closer vantage point. Did the guy have any remorse? Was he sitting there now, thinking of what he should have done? What he could have done differently? Would it matter if he was sorry for the past?

No. It doesn't matter. What's done is done.

Carl swung open the door, the hinges giving their familiar whine, and stood on the threshold. Kevin sat upright, the hammock stilling as he planted his feet firmly on the ground. His eyes widened as he peered at Carl, then he shot out of his seat and threw down his smoke.

"What the fuck are *you* doing here, kid?" Kevin adopted his usual pose—hands on hips, legs at ease—and expanded his chest.

Carl almost laughed. "Came back like I said I would."

Kevin chuckled. "Let me see now. What was it you said? That you were gonna *apply* the same thing to me as I'd done to you." He chuckled again and moved toward Carl, hands by his sides, fists bunched. "Well, we'll see about that."

Turning, Carl went back into the kitchen and yanked open a drawer, taking out a sturdy knife and holding it behind him. Kevin entered the room a moment later and slammed the back door, his ruddy face belying his anger. He flicked his head in an attempt to shift the lank lock of hair that had streaked across his face, but it didn't budge. With a huff, he brushed it back with his hand then took two paces toward Carl.

"You got a belt, kid?"

"Nope."

"Well? Don't you need one?"

"Nope."

"So how you gonna *apply* shit on me?" His laugh puffed out of that stinking mouth with its stained teeth and tongue yellowed from years of tobacco. Kevin stood like a wrestler, his arm muscles now soft from lack of exercise.

Amazing how a man can stay in shape from using a belt too often.

Carl gritted his teeth.

"You not gonna answer me, kid?"

Carl stared at him, at the bulging eyes that indicated Kevin teetered on the precipice, anger about ready to boil over.

"You'd better fuckin' answer me, or so help me God — "

Carl lunged forward and whipped the blade across Kevin's throat before the old man had a chance to register Carl's movement. Blood arced from the knife, splattering the filthy cream wall and the fingerprint-smudged fridge to their right. Kevin's eyes widened, and he staggered against the back door, hands raised to a gaping, blood-filled throat. His fingertips sank into the wound, and he slid down the door, his chest and vest front crimson. Gargles issued from the old man's throat, those ugly teeth bared in a grimace of pain. Carl watched, fascinated as the blood went from spewing to oozing with the stopping of Kevin's heart. He stepped toward his father and drew the knife back and forth over the unsullied, lower half of the vest to clean it, then turned and calmly exited the house. Knife still in hand, he strode across the road and unlocked the pickup, getting inside as though what had occurred...hadn't. After tossing the knife into the back seat, he started the truck then pulled away, intent on finding an out-of-the-way motel.

He headed back toward home—his real home—and pondered on how long it would take for Kevin to be discovered. Days. Possibly a week or two. A smile touched his lips while he imagined the stink of the old man's body as it bloated and began to decompose. Whoever found him had better have a strong stomach.

Carl laughed and picked up speed. He had the urge to fuck and fuck hard. He'd pay cash at a motel then venture into the next town in search of a clubber who needed release as much as he did.

Fuck, yeah!

Chapter Eight

I didn't have much of a choice. Vic stepped back, putting an appropriate amount of distance between us again. Oddly, the warmth his proximity had lent remained. I glanced up, and those deep brown eyes met mine.

"Ready?"

I shook my head, knowing all my desperation showed in my eyes. Carl always said I was too easy to read.

"I know." His voice had gone soft. "I know. I wish there was another way." He glanced over to the door of the station house then back to me. "I'm not going to let them railroad you. Promise." He wrapped gentle fingers around my arm, just above my elbow, and the absolute lack of force struck me as odd.

"You'll—you'll stay with me?"

"Right beside you. I'll process—" He clamped his mouth shut and frowned. "I'll do the paperwork and things."

"Process me."

We were mounting the stairs by then, and the building loomed, dark and slightly run-down.

"You'll process me." One thing I was beginning to understand about my life—it was just easier to call it how it was.

"It has to be done."

I nodded. "Then I want you to do it."

He pulled open the door then and maneuvered me inside ahead of him. It felt like procedure at that point. Hubbub inside made it hard to focus, and I held back, hoping for the reassurance of his bulk behind me. He grunted and gave me a light shove, just to keep me ahead of him. Was I supposed to act like a criminal? I wasn't anything but scared shitless.

"Over there."

He pointed past me to a desk in the far corner. Partial walls delineated the space, and as we approached I realized there were two desks, facing one another, and the other was occupied. The man sitting at it turned, stood, his eyes flashing.

"Where the hell have you been?"

"Calm down, Chewie."

I stifled a hysterical giggle. The guy was slightly hairier than average, and taller than Lil.

He made a low rumbling sound to go with his frown as he plopped back into his chair. "You should have called in. Who's this?"

"Mind your own homework." Vic pointed to the guy's desk, strewn with piles of forms and reports. "I'll put him through."

"You bring some punk in without calling for back-up, not even me, your own partner, and I'm not supposed to ask?"

"You're not supposed to ask," Vic agreed.

"That's him!" this exclamation, from behind Vic, brought Chewie back to his feet and turned Vic's head, but not before I saw the resignation on his face.

"Sit down, Colly," Vic snarled at the speaker. "I got it."

"Leave him," someone else said quietly, though the look I got from that cop scalded. "This is his collar."

I glanced at Vic, but his back was to me. "This isn't a collar," he said. "Not yet."

"Yet?" My voice might have squeaked. In fact, it did, and Vic spun back to me.

"Sit."

He pointed to the chair by his desk, and I sat, perched on the front edge to give my shackled hands room. From there, I had a good view of Vic glaring the rest of the men in the room down. He was playing his role of partner to the dead cop right to the hilt, but I could see the strain in the set of his shoulders and his tight grip on the back of his chair.

No one spoke.

Vic shifted his stance, spun his chair around, and turned his back on them. His gaze met mine. "I got this." Smooth, spare motions got him into his seat and the computer monitor adjusted and turned on. The questions came at me then, just as smooth. His tone was calm, cold, completely business, and he didn't once look away from his computer screen.

The questions were of the simple, name, rank and serial number variety. I answered them in tones I'm sure Vic couldn't hear, but he appeared to know enough about me. He didn't ask me to repeat myself, and I found a fair amount of time to sit there and wonder why his intimate knowledge of my life didn't disturb me as much as it should. It didn't even seem to be the right thing to be worrying about. Then again, I'd never been arrested before, or accused of murder. I had no idea what should be bothering me at that point.

I suppose I knew it was only a matter of time before someone else took an interest. Still, that someone shouting Vic's name across the room startled me. It only brought a resigned frown to Vic's face.

He drew his focus from the computer screen at last to fix it on Chewie. "Connelly?"

Chewie glanced up, and Vic tilted his head at me.

"Keep an eye on him."

"Bradley!" the shout came again, and Vic's shoulders scrunched up a bit.

Across the desk, Chewie—Connelly—nodded then shot me a dark glare. I slouched a little lower. The murmurs that drifted around swiveled heads in my direction. The room, preoccupied a moment before, rapidly turned cold and hostile. Beside me, Vic stood. His fingers twitched in my direction. His eyes flitted my way, his glance brief but easy to understand. *Stay still. Be quiet. Don't draw attention.*

I could do that.

"Comin', Cap." Vic headed off, twisting with supple grace through the maze of desks and skewed chairs, fielding curious stares and deflecting pointed questions.

"Why's he here?" someone asked.

"Put him in the damn cell and toss the key," came another gruff, bitter comment.

"Always by the book, ain't ya, Bradley?" This from a weasely man in dark denim and a tight T-shirt stretched over steroid-muscled arms crossed in front of himself. He stood and blocked Vic's way, chin thrust out, bulldog glare showing he didn't care that he barely came to Vic's shoulder. "We all know he did it. What's the point of all this?"

"Bradley!" His captain's voice cut through the thick vibe, and cops turned reluctantly back to whatever they'd been doing. All except the little man blocking Vic's way forward.

"What's it to you, Simpson? You never liked Jase anyway," Vic said.

"Like cop killers even less." The beefed-up little man turned his beady-eyed stare on me. "You think you'd get away with it, punk?"

I stared at him, mouth too dry to respond. I hardly resembled a punk by anyone's standards. Did I really come across like someone who could have killed a cop? Or anyone, for that matter? And the way the murder had been described. I shuddered. Carl had done that. More than once. Bile rose again. It surprised me I had anything left to throw up.

"Simpson." From a doorway somewhere to the left, a sharp female voice pinged off my awareness. "Come on, asshole. We have doors to knock on."

Someone else snickered, and the cop named Simpson shot Vic one last, venomous glare and swaggered off across the room. Vic glanced at me over his shoulder. I wasn't sure if I imagined the concern, or if he'd actually risked showing it. I knew I must have looked like complete shit, though, because Connelly shuffled some papers and grunted.

"You can ignore that jerk-off. He's got it in for just about everyone," Connelly said.

"Something specific with Vic?" I asked, trying to keep my voice conversational and not shaking, and failing miserably.

Connelly narrowed his eyes, but after a minute, he just answered the question, "He's an asshole. He's just a homo-fuckin'-phobic asshole." The words, growled out through his thick beard, made me shiver. His eyes, bright blue and penetrating, didn't waver from my face. "S'pose you've met your share of those."

"I guess." I watched him a moment, watching me, as though he was waiting for something from me. I had no idea what.

"You don't look like what I expected."

My breath caught. "What were you expecting?"

"He usually goes for more elfin-like, big-eyed hip sawyers."

"What?"

Connelly leaned forward, letting his gaze rove down over me then back to my face. "You're fit. Strong enough to take down a cop. The rest of them…" He shook his head. "Damn it if Vic isn't right about you, though. Tough on the outside, waif on the inside, I bet. Otherwise, I don't see why he's looking out for you. You didn't kill anyone."

"No! No, I didn't." I latched on to the thin branch of hope he was extending. "Why is this happening?"

"Evidence." He sighed and sat back in his chair. "Damnit, I wanted him to be wrong. I wanted this to be over." The pen he flung onto his desk bounced end over end and landed, rolling to rest against a coffee cup on Vic's desk with a little clink. "Would have been so much easier to talk him out of his crush than actually help him figure out a way to do this."

"Crush? Who? Figure out a way to do what?" If only everyone would stop talking in code and just tell me what the fuck had happened to my life.

"Shit." He was back to studying me again. "All right. Fine. We'll do it his way. Where's your boyfriend?"

"Carl?" I shifted uncomfortably. My arms ached. The

cuffs rattled behind me. "I don't know. I haven't seen him since yesterday. Last night."

"What time?"

"I don't know." I wasn't about to tell this guy I'd lost track of time while Carl worked me over, assaulted me, and left me tied up and helpless. That I had no idea how long I lay there wheezing and frightened he'd come back before I'd decided to get myself out was not something I was eager to share with the world. "Late, I guess."

He heaved a sigh so deep it ruffled the stiff hairs of his beard. "When I accepted this partnership, they warned me Vic was just broken. Freaked out over a dead partner and not thinking straight." Connelly leaned forward, sucked up a few of his beard hairs between his teeth, and watched me thoughtfully. "No one told me he's perfectly sane and right. No one wants to believe it."

"But you do, right? You believe I didn't do anything."

"What time did your boyfriend leave?" he asked again.

I shook my head, swallowed the bitter goop rising to the back of my mouth. "I don't know. After dark. Before the late nurse's shift." I shrugged helplessly. "I honestly don't know. Brian, my friend, picked me up, brought me back to his place before Lil went to work. I don't know what time it was."

"That's pretty vague."

"I—I'm sorry. I really don't know. Brian picked me up," I said again, repeating myself like it would somehow make things clearer. "We went to his. Lil went to work after I'd been there a while. I wasn't watching the clock."

"Well, where, when, and what you were doing is going to matter. Figure it out."

That's when Vic came back, face grim. He didn't speak as he reached down behind me and released my hands at last. The pins and needles in my arms were agony as I slowly moved them into a more natural position.

"Thank—"

He grunted, fastened the cuffs on my closest wrist again,

and drew it in front of me, motioning for the other hand. "Just a change of venues," he muttered, voice as dark as his expression. He pulled at the cuffs once he had them fastened, indicating I should get up and go with him. I didn't move.

Look at me. Please.

He did, finally. I'd somehow forgotten just how deep his eyes really were. I could see in there, though. He wasn't as sure now as he had been that it would be okay.

"Where are we going?" I asked.

"Questioning." Dull and flat, the word fell between us, and my insides fell with it.

"I didn't..." *Tell me you believe me.*

This time, he didn't read my mind. His eyebrows came down. He tugged at me again. "Come on."

"Victor?" Connelly's voice rumbled quietly under the hubbub of the room. "What's going on?"

"Questioning now. They're railroading." He didn't look at me. "I'm to bring him. They won't let me stay."

Connelly nodded. "Figured as much." He rose and yanked me up by one arm along with him. "Let's get this done, then."

They hauled me out of the room, down a grungy corridor where doors opened off each side at intervals. The floor tiles were coming up, and the paint was dull. Halfway down, they both stopped, and I was wedged between them.

"Who's doing it?" Connelly asked.

"Captain's looking for a volunteer. I expect he'll get more than a few."

"He will. I'll get us in there." Connelly wrinkled his brow in thought. "And by us, I mean me. We can't risk letting it get away from us." When Vic said nothing, Connelly made a sharp sound in his throat. "Vic. We can't let it get away from us, or we don't stand a chance of saving him. You get that, right?"

My blood ran cold and my palms began to sweat as I watched them discuss me like I wasn't in the room.

"I know," Vic snapped. "I fucking know. I don't like letting him out of my sight." He stared at me, making my skin warm under his scrutiny.

Connelly looked from him to me then back again. "Not that I think this is a good idea, but you had better not be wrong about this, Victor."

"I'm not wrong. Go."

Connelly was most of the way back to the squad room when Vic spoke again. "Jim."

Connelly turned, shook his head and said, "You're welcome." Then he disappeared back into the milling officers gathering around their captain.

"What did you say to him?" Vic swiveled me around to face him.

"Nothing. I—"

His frown was so dark it stopped me speaking.

Then I said, "He asked…where I was, what I did last night. He asked where Carl was."

"What did you tell him?" He enunciated every word, like I was too slow to understand.

"I don't know where Carl is. I was at home. Carl left, Brian came by later, picked me up—"

"How much later?"

I remembered the feeling of my arms slowly going numb, tied above my head, the sharp sting of the belt across my chest, the force, the fists. It was a long minute before I answered. "I don't know how much later. It was dark. Lil hadn't gone in for the night shift yet. He was at home when Bri and I got there. Lil bandaged me up." I held up my wrists as evidence. "Then it was a while before he left for work."

"How long?"

"I don't know!"

He shook his head. "Why doesn't anyone ever look at a clock?"

"Everything would be so much easier for you," I muttered.

His eyebrows went up in surprise. He actually chuckled.

"It fucking would be."

I followed his quick glance down the hall, then back the way we'd come to the door Jim Connelly had closed behind him. We were alone.

Vic rested a hand on my shoulder. "You listen to me, Paul. Whatever they ask, you stick to facts. Tell the truth."

"But—" I weighed the humiliation of telling him against the chance they would see reason without my ever divulging all the gory details. "I don't remember the time. I don't even know if I actually slept at Bri's after Lil left. I don't know what time I got up this morning. I don't. You said you'd be there."

"But I have to follow orders, and right now orders say no."

"What? In the interests of a fair trial?" I scoffed.

"In the interests of clearing this up without more scandal to the department."

"That's not good for me."

Vic's face went bleak again. I didn't like that dark look on his features. It didn't suit him.

"No. That's not good for you. But lying, holding back, will only make it seem like you've got something to hide, and that will be worse for you."

I nodded. I'd gone a little numb to the shock of what was happening to me. I couldn't even contemplate how long I'd been sleeping with a murderer. How many times after Jason died had I taken Carl back when I knew he was bad for me? Bad for a whole lot of people, it turned out. "Do you know what happened to Carl?"

"Believe me, Paul, if I knew where he was, he would be here and not you."

"No. I mean before. Do you know why? Why is he...the way he is?"

"Who knows? Because he was younger than you when his abuse started? His father was more vicious than yours? He didn't have a Brian in his life?" Vic shook his head. "Who knows why people do what they do. Why they fall for the wrong people."

He turned me so I couldn't help but look at him, and once again find myself and simultaneously lose myself in those eyes.

"Or the right ones," he added.

My gut clenched and this time, it had nothing to do with fear. This sensation was wholly different from being sick over Carl. "Vic?"

"You listen to me." He moved his hand from my shoulder to the back of my neck where he left it, warm and strong.

I could feel a callous on his palm, the pads of his fingers resting just behind my ear.

"Even if they don't let me in, I will be right on the other side of the glass. Jim will be in there with you. We won't let them manipulate you. Whatever happens."

He pulled, and I stumbled.

It wasn't odd to lay my head against his chest. It should have been. My cuffed hands were pressed between us, trapped against the firm muscle of his thigh. He ran little circles over the side of my neck with his thumb.

"Your partner says I'm not really your type." I couldn't think of anything else to say in that fantastic moment, so divorced from reality.

Vic's rumble vibrated right through me. "I don't know what happened, Paul. I don't even know you, except what I've observed watching Carl, and what Brian and Lil have told me."

I waited for him to say something else, but he seemed to be finished.

"Why do I trust you?" I tried to tell myself I'd trusted Carl, too, and look how that had turned out. But no, what Vic inspired was something Carl had never given me – calm. Even cuffed and terrified, right then, in that hallway, I felt safe, and it wasn't a feeling I was at all used to. It wasn't just because he had a badge, either. My father had been a cop. He'd also been an over-stressed, lonely, volatile man full of dangerous edges and hidden traps.

"You can trust me. And you can trust Chewie. Jim. Let him help. Listen to him."

"I want you there." For the barest moment, I worried it sounded pathetically frightened the way I'd said that, but then, when he stroked his hand down my back, I found I didn't care if it did. "I can't…"

"Yes, you can. Just tell the truth. As much of it as you can, as accurately as you can."

"You don't understand." I would have tried to catch his eye, make him see I was serious, but what I had to say next I could barely say out loud, never mind while I watched his expression change from helpful to horrified at how much of an idiot I actually was. "I can't tell them what he did." The memory of the cold hate in homophobic Simpson's eyes sent a chill through me. "Before he left." I swallowed hard then took in a deep breath, afterward spilling it all out as fast as I could. Still the words left the acrid taste of fear and anger on my tongue and an empty pit of loathing in my belly.

Vic had stopped moving his hand. His entire body was stiff. He said nothing for too long.

I twisted from him. "You see?" I asked, bitterness spitting out over him with the words, "And you're supposed to be on my side. I can't tell them that." Then I realized the expression on his face wasn't disgust. It wasn't horror that I'd let it happen. It was rage, and it wasn't directed at me. "Vic?" I stepped farther back. I knew that twist of features too well. My father, Carl—they wore that mask a lot.

Vic didn't actually let me out of his grasp. His face was a grimace of anger but it softened almost immediately when I pulled at his grip, frantic to get away. He let me go, but I didn't move.

He cupped my face with his free hand, tipped it up so I couldn't turn away from him. "That's just something else I'll make him pay for, one way or another."

"Please don't." I didn't want that twisted expression on his face, ever. "I just want it all over."

He nodded. "Me too. I know it's hard, but you can't not tell them."

"Hard?" I wanted to turn my back on him, but I couldn't make myself.

"Impossible, then. But you have to. The whole truth. He's the one who did this. He put you here. I know it. I just have to prove it. They have to know what kind of a man he is. When the proof comes, it will be that much easier to convince them."

"And what if the proof never comes? What if he just never shows up?"

"Paul, he will. Because the one thing a guy like that can never stomach is to lose the thing he sees as his greatest treasure, the thing he thinks he's doing it all for. He won't run away without you."

I wanted to be sick all over again. The thought that Carl did any of those things because of me turned my stomach. Maybe Vic saw that in my face, maybe he misinterpreted it. I didn't know.

He just hugged me close again and whispered, "You're safe. I am not letting him close. He won't touch you ever again."

Like I was a damsel, needing his protection. I had no desire to be the pathetic creature who longed to believe that kind of promise, who needed it, but there it was. And I did want to believe it. I did want to hide there inside his arms and never come out. Of course, I couldn't stay there. Too soon he was moving back, clearing his throat, and leading me off down the hall and into a small room with a one-way glass wall, a table and chairs, and all I could think was how much it shouldn't remind me of every movie set and every cop show I'd ever seen.

In the end, they didn't let him in, and maybe that was better for both of us. If he'd had to stand there while I recited everything Carl had said and done the night before, and he'd had to watch me reveal every bruise while in the same room, I don't know if either one of us would have been able to remain calm. I'd seen his distress over how Carl had treated me twice now, and I didn't think he could hide it. I didn't see how Vic's feelings could be interpreted as good for either my case or his career. And after Connelly had drilled me through the horrific scene for the third time, I had to suspect he'd deliberately placed Vic on the other side of that glass to protect his partner, at least, if not me.

After the tenth, twelfth — I'd lost count — time I'd told my story, and they'd prodded for more details, some trip-up to latch on to, I was so tired I could barely think straight. I almost didn't notice the urgent knock on the door when it came.

It was Vic, hurtling inside, his face completely too pale to be good. "Jim."

Connelly pursed his lips, turned his head. "What?" Maybe he was tired too. Maybe he just liked being surly and difficult with Vic.

"I need you. We have to go to the hospital. There's been another victim. Brian Jacobs. Only this time the bastard missed. He didn't quite kill him."

There was a lot of commotion after that. A lot of white noise I didn't hear after Vic had said Brian's name, in conjunction with 'victim', 'hospital', and 'not quite dead'.

"We have our guy, Bradley." This buzzed through my mind fog from the other cop, Simpson, who had been backing up Connelly's questions with more and nastier ones of his own. He pointed at me. "You brought him in yourself. We just have to find the hole in his story."

"There's no hole," I insisted.

Simpson stood. "You go ahead and believe that." He turned his back on me. Clearly, I was nothing to him but a bit of grunge someone had dragged into his presence. He turned his glare on Connelly, ignoring Vic with the same disdain he'd shown me throughout. "We have enough to book him, and you know it. Go on ahead, off on your little expedition. We're done here anyway." He took hold of me then and dragged me to my feet, sticking his face too close to mine. "We'll figure out where the lies are, punk. Don't think we won't."

He was towing me out. Past Vic, still too pale, and Connelly, tired, frustrated and clearly furious with everyone.

"Wait!" I hauled myself free of Simpson's grip and turned to where Vic was already hurrying away. "What about Brian?" I called after him. "What happened?"

Vic glanced back, stopped, and I saw his fists were tight, his shoulders hunched forward. "I don't know. I have to go find out. Paul…"

I clenched my teeth. He had to leave me there. There was no choice. If Brian was hurt, he had to go and find out what happened. I nodded. Simpson was dragging me away, not back to the squad room, but deeper into the building.

He wasn't gentle about tossing me into a cell populated with a few surly men. "Have fun with this one, assholes," he told them, talking about me like I was nothing more than a useless dog for them to torment. They leered at me, managing to appear both bored and menacing at once.

He tapped the opening in the barred door, reclaiming my attention. "I'll take those cuffs now." A nasty grin spread over his face as he glanced past me, to the men sprawled in the cell behind me. "Or would you rather keep 'em? I hear you like it that way."

I stuck my hands through the slot without lifting my eyes to his ruddy face.

"Say please," he said.

"Fuck you."

Complete silence greeted my outburst, forcing me to glance up. The nasty grin only widened as he peeled his lips back from his teeth, and his eyes gleamed meanly. It was a far more frightening expression than anything I'd seen on Carl's face. There was no rage there, no manic disregard for me. It was just calculated, premeditated cruelty.

"Think you got your pronouns mixed there. I'm sure someone will be pleased to open up that pretty ass of yours, freak." He made no move to unlock the manacles.

Pride had kept my mouth shut through the worst of what Carl could throw at me. He was one man, and something still human in him had stopped him before he'd ever hurt me beyond forgiveness. There was none of that here. A quick glance over my shoulder at the men lounging against the bars told me that, acting or not, it didn't matter what I did or didn't say. I was screwed.

"Please." The worst part was not being able to meet his eye.

Snickers all round.

God. Fuck, let these assholes be posers.

This was a police lock-up, not high-security prison. They were here for misdemeanors, public displays of drunkenness, petty theft. God, I hoped so.

For a split second, I thought he would walk away, leaving me there, cuffed and helpless. He didn't, but the roughness he employed to free me opened up the cuts on my wrist — I felt the thin scabs peel away beneath the bandages. I had the irrational thought that the scent of blood would mark me as easy prey. Irrational, because I was pretty sure there were a lot of things about me that marked me out even without that.

I made a point of ignoring the other men. They made a point of watching my every move. I felt like an idiot, but I kept my back to the bars anyway, and glared through rows of cells to the window at the farthest end of the room. The sky was dull, gray and overcast, and from where I sat, I watched the last of the grungy light fade away. All through the cavernous room, sounds of voices and laughter floated. Lights had been turned down, enough to make it hard to see beyond the next few cells, but it wasn't exactly dark. This was a small taste, I knew. Nothing compared to what it could be like, *would* be like, if Vic didn't manage to make them understand that I was telling the truth.

Please. Fuck. Let him figure it out.

I picked absently at the ragged bandages as time passed. My cell mates speculated loudly and lewdly as to how and why I happened to have acquired them in the first place. I kept quiet. Dinner was brought, though I didn't eat much, or argue when one of the others took my tray before I was done.

Vic will fix this. I kept telling myself that as I watched the bruiser eat my meal. It was one meal. The only meal I would miss for being here — Vic was not going to let this happen.

It must have been some sort of signal, because as soon as the dishes were gone the scathing speculation about my sexual practices quickly escalated. I crouched with my back pressed hard against the bars in one corner of a bunk and hoped to hell it wasn't going to turn physical.

That's when Connelly appeared. His huge form striding down the row of cells turned my roomies as docile as lambs well before he got to our door. He made quick work of getting the guard to open it.

"Come on." He nodded at me. "Someone here to pick you up."

Just like that, it was over. I glanced at the far away window and the deep gray-brown of evening lit by orange streetlights.

"Who?" It couldn't be Vic, or he would have come down here himself. At least, I had the sudden revelation that I hoped he would. Brian was apparently in hospital, and if so, Lil would be there too. I didn't know anyone else who cared enough.

"Let's go," was all Connelly said.

It wasn't like I was going to quibble. I followed him back down the long, echoing hallway, away from the jeers, toward freedom.

Chapter Nine

The motel stank of stale liquor and cigarette smoke. Carl had stopped off to buy some new clothes, lube and condoms before finding this shithole and signing in using another of Paul's credit cards. He switched on the light and gazed around, disgusted by the squalor. It reminded him of where he'd just been and everything he strove to get away from. He wanted things clean, orderly, right. He laughed, the sound dry and without feeling.

Fucking irony. Gotta love it.

Okay, so he liked things clean, yet he risked getting sullied by blood every time he gave in to that all-consuming urge inside him. If he thought about it, he'd formed a pattern with that. Getting dirty then getting clean afterward. Yeah, he liked that analogy.

He dumped his bags beside the double bed.

Shit, doesn't this place have a maid?

Yeah, it'd been given a cursory clean, but it wasn't to his standards.

Still, beggars can't be choosers and all that crap.

He needed to sleep for a while before heading out to find a giving asshole who'd help assuage the raging need throbbing in his balls. No good picking someone up when he wasn't at his best. Fatigue led to mistakes, and he couldn't allow that. No, despite his desire to ram his cock inside a guy tied up with his belt, he'd have to wait.

A wave of lethargy swept over him, and he flopped onto the bed, hands braced behind his head. The aroma of dust and unwashed bodies wafted up, and he closed his eyes, blocking out thoughts of dirty beds and how often the sheets were cleaned in this place. He'd shower after his nap anyway, and once he returned home he could have a good soak to rinse away the filth he'd encountered on this trip.

Filth. Fucking right. This trip had been full of it.

But I'm doing it for Paul.

He pondered on whether Paul had been picked up by the cops yet.

He'll be so damn pleased to hear I've offered bail to get him out when I go back.

A smile curved his mouth at his thoughts of their reunion, how Paul would lean on him for support.

I'll take him to his place and show him a different kind of love. Yeah, and he'll be up for it, being so grateful and all.

Carl dozed, too hyped to sleep properly but his body needing the respite, and he revisited the last few hours in his more lucid moments. Damn, Kevin finally being gone had given him freedom. It winged through him like a tangible thing, a drug that rivaled any on the underground market. He should have done this years ago. If only he'd known how good it would feel.

So fucking free, like the past has gone and I'm here with a clean slate.

Time passed, and he opened his eyes to glance at his watch. Yep, late enough now to hit the shower then visit a club. Rejuvenated by his musings, he got up and headed to the bathroom, disrobing along the way. He turned the dial and waited for the water to heat — too much to expect instant warmth in a hellhole like this — then climbed into the tub. He soaped up with the cheap, unscented shower gel left by a previous customer and used it to wash his hair. With the water pattering over his body, he went over everything he'd done, the need to make sure he hadn't messed up paramount.

I left Brian's and I — Brian. Shit.

Would the guy have called the cops on him? He didn't think Brian had the balls.

But Lil does.

Heart rate soaring, he stumbled from the tub then skidded out of the bathroom to scoop up his dirty shirt. After drying himself with it, he rushed to the bag of new clothes and took them out, ripping off tags and dressing fast. He pulled on his boots then stuffed his other clothes into the bag, glancing around to make sure he hadn't left anything behind. He laughed wryly.

If I think I haven't left anything behind, I'm retarded.

Quickly, he took the blanket from the bed by its four corners and yanked open the motel door, flapping the material out into the night, praying any hairs or skin flakes would come off. Back inside, he grabbed the pillow and repeated his actions, inspecting it to make sure it was clean.

Fuck it, just take the damn things with you.

Jamming the blanket and pillow under his arm and picking up his bag, he went outside then threw them into the back seat of his vehicle, slamming the door before going back inside.

Back in the bathroom he unhooked the showerhead from the wall and switched on the water. He swirled the bath in the sporadic stream until he figured he'd washed all trace of himself far down the pipes, then wiped the showerhead with tissue. Bathroom clean. Or, at least as clean as he was going to get it.

Finally, as a last touch he covered his hand with the bottom of his new shirt and proceeded to mock-polish every surface whether he'd touched the damn things or not. Satisfied he'd covered his ass, he picked up the discarded clothes tags and left the room, closing the door by hooking his boot around the bottom.

Done. Back in control. Good. He got behind the wheel, gripped it tight with his forearms resting on the cool plastic, and took a deep breath. Mentally, he retraced his steps inside that room just in case he'd missed anything. He hadn't, but something nagged at the edges of his brain, gnawing with sharp teeth but not allowing him to grasp on to it and work out what he'd done wrong.

Think. Think, god damn it! The momentary calm of control crumbled away under the biting worry he'd made a mistake.

He stared at the closed motel door and thought. Thought so hard his head hurt, throbbing right along with those teeth that kept biting, nibbling, irritating.

The credit card. I used Paul's card when he's probably in jail. Shit, shit, shit!

He shoved the stick into reverse and stomped on the gas, screeching the pickup in a backward arc, then slamming into drive. He sped across the car park, his heart beating so fast his head lightened as he jerked to a stop in the exit. Cars zoomed past on the highway. Too many of them for him to pull out. He cursed, palms and brow sweating, and clenched and unclenched the steering wheel. He stared left then right. It looked like a gap was coming up. If he was quick he could nip between two cars. A flashing light blipped about five cars down, and his stomach muscles spasmed, real fear gripping him for the first time since he'd started this shit.

Fuck. Cops. The card. Why the hell did I use it? Why didn't I think?

He smacked the wheel with the heel of his hand, the horn giving a short bark of protest. The sound jolted him into action, and he took the chance and skidded out of the exit, easing between two cars. More horns blared, and he slowed in case the cops behind caught sight of his pickup speeding along the highway. He tensed, tighter and tighter as he darted his attention back and forth between the rear-view mirror and the road ahead. Finally, he let out a ragged breath as the cop car turned into the motel parking lot, its lights dousing.

He was safe. For now.

Getting his nerves under control, Carl drove on, contemplating changing his plans. He nodded, mentally talking to himself about what he should do next.

The next town is too close. Fuck it, I'll head for the one after that. Clubs will still be open by the time I get there.

He frowned at the voice of his conscience that asked, *You sure you ought to go?*

Fuck, yeah, I'm sure. They'll be looking for me, I dig that, but what I plan to do won't take long. Pick up some guy, go back to his place, do what I've got to do, then leave. I can manage that, right?

He nodded again.

Yeah, I can manage that.

* * * *

The club had its own car park, and Carl wedged the pickup between a Ford Focus and a Subaru situated at the rear, bushes overhanging the bumpers. He'd calmed on his journey, forcing himself to concentrate on what lay ahead. He coached himself one final time before reaching into his bag and rooting around for a baseball cap, his flick knife, the lube and the packet of three. Cap on, he slid his stuff in the back pocket of his jeans. Got out of his vehicle. Locked up and studied the area from the shadows. Cameras mounted at the top of tall poles in the far corners were directed at the car park. Others lower down appeared to point to the outside of the club, probably to catch any violent action from drunken revelers. He eyed the higher cameras. What did he care if they'd caught images of the pickup coming in? It wasn't his, and he doubted the cops this far away from where he'd stolen it were aware it was in their town.

He walked toward the club, cap pulled low over his brow. He supposed he looked like any average Joe. His features below the cap peak could belong to a thousand or more people. No, he didn't need to worry. He'd be in and out so quick no one would remember him anyway.

The neon signed beckoned, luring him, an echoing voice inside his head urging him forward. He could do this.

Damn right I can.

Thankful no queue snaked outside, he walked right in, head down, the beefy men either side of the door giving him no attention. After paying the bored-looking woman at the entry booth with cash, he took the stairs two at a time, the tiny, flashing strings of lights along the riser widths promising fun and good times. He thought back to the past, to other nights and other clubs where he'd acted like a regular guy, before he'd met Paul and had been consumed by a love so strong that Kevin's teachings had come crashing through. He grimaced and ousted the memories from his mind, needing to keep his head clear and his senses keen. No way could he let his concentration slip. He'd already messed up enough today as it was.

At the top, a packed club greeted him. Bodies gyrated to jungle music, inebriated people throwing away their inhibitions to dance with arms waving, heads nodding. They seemed like they were on drugs too — a lot of them, several lines of coke or a few upper pills. Carl didn't give a shit — if he could find someone out of their skull on illegal substances, all the better.

The beat pulsed through him, exacerbating the tingle in his balls. He stood still for a moment to soak that feeling in, stopping his thoughts only when his cock started getting hard. Then he weaved through drinkers, studying the crowd for a lonely dude who'd be grateful for his attention. Spying one sitting in a corner booth, he slid onto the seat beside him and prayed he was gay. If he wasn't, well, he'd find man who was. There had to be another queer among so many people.

"All right?" Carl shouted at him over the music.

His booth buddy nodded, giving him a weird glance and shifting away. What, did Carl smell or something? Wasn't he good-looking enough for this prick?

Try again. Harder.

"Great place, yeah?" Carl asked, smiling so he'd hopefully be perceived as no one to be wary of.

Nodding absently, the guy stared at the crowd, jaw clenching. Carl followed his gaze and spotted a blonde woman staggering their way, a bottle in one hand and a clutch bag in the other. She arrived at the booth then plopped down beside the man, pressing her lips against his cheek, kneading his crotch with slender fingers.

Fuck.

Carl eased out of the booth then headed for the bar. He didn't want a drink—*fingerprints, gotta think of the fingerprints*—so stood beside it, watching the throng. The thought arose that he maybe wouldn't find anyone here, that his mission would be thwarted by the lack of the other player needed to act out the next scene. What would he do then? Convince a straight man that dipping his wick with someone of the same sex was considered hip these days? Or should he move on? Drive to another town? There was no way Carl would settle for just jacking off. He had to feel skin on skin to attain the ultimate high.

A hot wisp of breath heated his neck, and he turned to face a man about his height, wiry-framed and handsome in a Ben Affleck kind of way. Carl frowned, for a moment uncomprehending that this Ben-a-like was interested in him.

"Lonely?" the man asked, head tilted, his honest eyes regarding Carl.

"A little," Carl said. "Came out to find... Well, yeah, you know how it is."

"Good job I do," he said. "Greg." He held out his hand for shaking. "You?"

Carl shook it. "John. My name's John."

"Aren't they all?" Greg grinned. "Come on. My place or yours?"

"Yours." Carl smiled and followed Greg down the stairs and out into the night.

And he scores! Just like that. Fuck, I'm good.

In the pickup, Carl tailed Greg, filing away the turns and street names so he'd remember the route back to the highway.

Let's see if his confidence falters once we get to his place. Let's see if he's so in control then.

Carl laughed, giddy from the thrill of acting out his desires. Everything fell into place every time, and he mused on whether a higher calling directed his life. He didn't believe in God—no, he couldn't, not when Kevin had brought him up the way he had. God would have stopped those horrors, surely. But there could be something else orchestrating his life, couldn't there? Angels and demons or whatever?

He tapped the steering wheel at a red light, staring at Greg's rear fender, eyes glazing. He contemplated every scenario that could possibly lie ahead, working through his actions and reactions, ensuring he knew exactly what to do should something go wrong. And it could, he knew that, but refused to fully believe it.

How could things go wrong when they felt so right?

He was in control. He had it all covered. He was the best.

It took a honking horn to pull him from his reverie, and he pressed on the gas to catch up to Greg's car, which turned into an underground parking lot. As far as Carl could make out, no security cameras were in sight. He maneuvered into a spot beside Greg's then got out, smiling as he trailed the man to an elevator. Their footsteps echoed, the sound bouncing off the walls, giving the place an eerie feel. Carl felt as though he starred in a movie of his own making, the actor everyone adored because he was so good at what he did.

God, I love this shit!

The elevator arrived quickly and they stepped inside, Carl scanning the interior for cameras.

None. Good.

Greg jabbed his thumb onto the level three button and the elevator rose with a judder. They didn't look at one another—they both knew this was a one-night stand that didn't need the added mess of inane conversation—but Carl studied Greg's reflection in the metal door. The man stared up at the ceiling and tapped his foot.

Easy to bring down. Easy to manipulate. Look at him fiddling with his pants leg. Nervous. Just the way I like them.

Greg bit his bottom lip, and it turned Carl on even more. That vulnerability, that small gesture showing that Greg maybe wasn't completely sure about what he was doing. Or perhaps he was pondering on how Carl would view his body, whether Carl would think him desirable or not. Whether his cock was up to scratch — was it long enough, thick enough, and would it get hard enough?

Gone were the days when Carl had thought the same things. And Greg's days of thinking them would be over soon too.

Carl had to stop himself from chuckling.

The elevator lurched to a stop and a ping sounded as the doors opened. Carl walked behind Greg to door number sixteen then followed him inside. His prey strode to the second door on their left down a long hall. Carl peeked inside a living room to his right, noting a state-of-the-art flat-screen TV and an expensive black leather sofa.

What does this guy do for a living?

He closed his mind off from caring. What did it matter? He had a job to get done, a need that needed sating, and what Greg did or didn't do in the workplace was no concern of Carl's. He walked down the hallway then turned, eyeing the bedroom while feeling his back pocket. The knife bulged pleasantly under the fabric, and Carl smiled.

His cock bloated a bit. God, just the thought of what was about to happen was enough for Carl to get his rocks off. He schooled his mind so it wasn't racing too far ahead into the future. He kind of wanted to savor this. Then again, if it went too quickly, so what? There were plenty more men he had to get rid of. Plenty more times he could feel this way. For Paul. To make sure Paul never went with any of them.

So Carl stood in the doorway and watched as Greg undressed hurriedly then draped his clothes on a chair in the corner. His cock already hard, Greg smiled sheepishly at Carl before turning to face the window above the bed. Buttocks that were ripe for a thrashing clenched, and Carl swallowed, realizing with regret that despite wanting to drag this out, he didn't really have the time to indulge in such pleasures.

Get in, get out. That's the deal you made with yourself. Deviate from the plan and you risk fucking up.

"Got a belt?" Carl asked.

Greg spun to face him, a fleeting dash of shock crossing his face before he masked it with bravado. "Yeah. Sure. You into kink?"

"Damn right I am." Carl laughed to ease away any misgivings Greg might be having. "You?"

Greg pulled a belt from the loops in his pants, seemingly feigning nonchalance. "Not tried it, but I'm open to new experiences."

Oh, you'll be having a new experience all right.

Carl stifled a chuckle and held his hand out for the belt. The leather felt good in his palm, and he enjoyed the rush of blood to his cock. "You want me to take charge, right?"

Greg nodded, the flush of desire tinting his cheeks. His cock twitched.

"Giver or a taker?" Carl moved to the bottom of the bed.

Taker if ever I fucking saw one.

"Taker."

"Right." Carl nodded. "Get on the bed, face down."

Greg obeyed, his arms by his sides, cheek pressed to the mattress, eyes looking right.

Carl climbed on the bed and straddled him. "Hands up to the headboard."

After lifting his arms, Greg curled his fingers around an iron pole.

Carl leaned forward and secured Greg's wrists then tied the belt to the pole. "I'll make you feel fucking *good*," he whispered in Greg's ear, flicking his tongue out to taste the lobe. He changed position and kneeled between Greg's open legs. He reached to his back pocket to bring out the knife, lube and condoms. Carl placed the blade within easy reach to his left. Jerking down his zip, he freed his erection, giving it a bit of a hard yank.

Fuck, that feels good.

He rolled on a condom, hating the damn feel of it, but knowing it was a necessary precaution. Lubing the condom, he then slapped Greg's buttock — hard — and waited for the red stain of his handprint to appear. When it did, he smiled, satisfied with how easily he could mark someone. "Lift up. Kneel."

Greg did so. Carl's cock thickened further, and he smoothed his hands over Greg's ass cheeks, closing his eyes to convince himself it was Paul he caressed, Paul he would fuck. Touching his cock to get lube on his thumb, he opened his eyes then circled Greg's asshole, pushing his thumb inside to ready the man for the fuck of his life. Greg gave a low whimper, spurring Carl on to loosening that ass quickly. Carl's cock ached, and a steady pulse beat at the base of his balls. He couldn't wait. The excitement of his day had been too much, and he needed the release. After removing his thumb, he butted his cock to Greg's asshole, pushing inside harder than he should have but uncaring of any pain he caused. Greg grunted, and Carl ignored him, gripping Greg's waist and thrusting in to the hilt.

"Ah, fuck! Careful, man!" Greg said through gritted teeth.

Fuck you.

Carl eased in and out, slowly at first, and not because of any consideration for Greg either. No, he went slow because he liked it that way, liked the anticipation of speeding up then fucking hard and fast. The moment came when he couldn't hold back any longer, and he pumped that ass with an unforgiving rhythm, pleased to hear Greg's moans.

"Yeah, I'm making you feel good, baby," Carl ground out, his cock vein pulsating. "Ah, yeah, I love you, Paul. Fucking love you!"

Cum spurted from him, the heady rush of his orgasm spacing him out, sending him into a swirl of bliss he could've drowned in. He scrunched his eyes closed, another ejaculation coming out so fast his cock hole hurt, and he reveled in it. Fucking reveled in pumping Paul's ass.

Showing Paul who that tight little hole of his belonged to. He slowed, glorying in the aftershocks and cock twitches, then gave a short, sharp thrust to expel the last of his cum. He opened his eyes and pulled out. Shoved his condom-covered cock in his pants. Zipped up, rage overtaking the pleasure he'd so recently experienced.

"You didn't like that?" Carl asked. "You didn't like me calling you Paul?"

Greg hunched up the bed, a ball of flesh at the headboard, the look he flung over his shoulder one of bewilderment tinged with hatred. "It was weird, man. Fucking weird."

"Weird? *Weird?*" Carl snatched up his flick knife, red rage thundering through him. "I'll give you fucking weird!"

Grabbing a fistful of Greg's hair, he yanked his head back, exposing his neck. He clicked the knife open out of its sheath then pressed the blade against skin and the pulsing vein in Greg's throat. He sliced, wanting this guy to die quickly, the bastard undeserving of Carl wasting Paul's name on him. He let go of his hair, ignoring the gurgles and Greg's bucking body, and got off the bed, anger still roiling through him.

Lube and condom wrapper back in his pocket, he sneered and left the room, past caring if his fingerprints were on that belt. Storming down the hallway, he raged as he slammed out of the apartment, poking at the elevator button with a shirt-covered finger. The contradiction wasn't lost on him. Leaving his fingerprints at the scene but not in the elevator? He should be worried about his mental state, but he recognized he was too far gone to analyze it properly right now.

It was time to go home. Time to save Paul. Time to be a hero. *That* was what mattered.

Chapter Ten

"Connelly?" It didn't feel right to call him Jim, and certainly not Chewie. Not out loud. I didn't know him well enough—hadn't earned that right. And he was so much older than me—I should have called him Mr. Detective, maybe. But that realization came too late.

He was frustratingly closed-mouthed. All I wanted was a name. Who was here to get me?

Fucking hell, don't let it be Carl.

The thought stopped me in my tracks. "Detective Connelly?" I wanted to demand, but the name came out a feeble question.

He walked on ahead of me without a word. I might not have even been there.

"You people always keep this place so damn cold?" I muttered. I wrapped my arms around my waist, not sure exactly what I was trying to protect myself from. Silence, maybe, the chill, myriad other things I didn't want to think about.

At least that made him stop, too. "Is it cold?" he asked, disinterested as he turned away again and resumed walking. He opened the door at the end of the same hallway Vic had led me down what felt like a week ago. "I hadn't noticed."

I wondered what he *did* notice. But there was no use standing there like an idiot. I had to go, had to take the chance at getting the hell out of here, whoever had come for me. If it was Carl, I'd...do...something.

With a sigh, I made my feet move, one after the other, down the hallway that stretched like something out of nightmare I would never reach the end of.

It was no warmer in the squad room. The place resembled a deserted battlefield. We passed through the maze of disorganized desks, strewn with unfinished paperwork, in silence. The few cops there watched my progress with almost the same hostility they'd greeted me with earlier. I supposed they didn't like their bird in hand being released when they hadn't managed to flush the bushes for the real killer.

I shivered again. Odd. Why could I only remember the good times spent with Carl, suddenly? The Carl I'd first met had been gentler, comfortingly possessive. Not a man who brutally murdered for no good reason. Why hadn't I noticed the change? Or maybe there hadn't been one. Maybe I was just that blind.

"Wait here." Connelly pointed to the chair beside his desk.

I sat, shoving my hands into my jeans pockets. Not that it was any help in warming them. I couldn't stop the shivering.

Connelly returned a minute or so later with papers which he shoved across the desk in front of me, along with a pen.

"What?" I said.

"Sign." He watched me, steady, unblinking.

"What is it?"

"Release papers. I'd advise you to read anything you have to sign." He leaned forward slightly. "The one bit of evidence we had, that they were willing to convict on, has just been thrown into enough doubt that they can't hold you."

"What do you mean?" No one had ever told me what that one piece of evidence was.

"They found a credit card — your credit card — at one of the crime scenes."

"That's impossible! I wasn't there..." But then, I didn't have to be. The only other person who might have had access to my credit cards *had* been there.

"What?" He leaned a little closer. "You remember

something?"

"Yeah." I swallowed hard as a chill seeped beyond a surface shiver deep into my bones. "Carl took my wallet when he l-left me...you know. When Bri came to take me back to his, I noticed my wallet was gone. I just thought..."

"Thought what?"

"He did that sometimes. Carl. He took my keys and my wallet when he left. So I couldn't go anywhere." And fuck. How pathetic did that sound?

But Connelly just nodded, face impassive, as though he'd heard it all before. Likely, he had.

"What happened to change their minds?" I asked.

Connelly sighed. "While you were freezing your ass off in a cell full of −" He stopped, curled his lip and started over. "While you were in custody, someone checked into a hotel three towns over, using your credit card. That puts at least one of your cards into someone else's hands. Couple it with your story, and with Leland's story that you were at their place − he calls himself Lil, though, right? − and there's nothing to hold you on. Some of my...colleagues aren't happy about that."

I slumped back in my chair. "So he left." Carl might have inadvertently cleared me, but he wasn't, as Vic thought, coming back for me. I should not have felt loss at that. I pushed Carl and my confused feelings for him aside. I didn't want him back. I didn't want him. "What happens to him if...?"

"If he did it? If they prove it?" Connelly drew his eyebrows down. "You care?"

I shrugged. Did I?

He leaned farther forward in his chair. "That Leland guy was right. You really do love this maniac."

"Lil, he doesn't go by Leland anymore." I don't know why I felt compelled to point that out. Avoidance maybe.

Connelly just sat back in his chair. It creaked under his shifting weight, the sound loud in the quiet room. "I'm sure at some point there will be more questions for you to answer. Try not to forget anything else."

Thank whatever twisted god was ruling my life he hadn't pressed for some coherent accounting of how I felt about Carl. I didn't know myself, and it didn't help that even the bruises weren't enough to keep me focused on the bad times. And everything else had begun to bleed into more recent thoughts of Vic, his strong arms and incredible eyes. That was some fucked-up momentum that allowed me to turn from one to the other so fast.

"So."

That hard voice hammering the one word against the back of my neck shocked me out of my thoughts. There was no mistaking the hostility. This same cop, Simpson, who had challenged Vic had spent hours countering all of Connelly's questions and scoffing at my answers. Belittling me. I didn't bother to acknowledge him.

He leaned a fist on the papers in front of me, bending so his stale coffee breath wafted into my face. "They're lettin' you out."

"I didn't do anything," I mumbled, hating how my voice fell and that I cringed away from him.

"So you said."

"Leave it, Simpson."

"So how does it happen you get yourself tied to the bed in the first place, huh?" The asshole was relentless.

"I said leave it!" Connelly yanked the Simpson away from his desk.

"Serves him right. Keeping that kind of company," Simpson said.

"I didn't know —"

"What kind of man he is?" Simpson pulled out of Connelly's grasp and hovered over me again. "How could you not? You sleep with something that tainted, it affects you. Don't try to tell me different." He glared me down, ignoring Connelly, the other cops, some commotion off toward the front of the office, and waited.

What he was waiting for, I couldn't say.

"You can't just walk in here!"

I don't know who shouted that. It was enough to break the stalemate, though. Simpson glanced up. Connelly's lips twitched. The clack-clack of hard-soled shoes on the floor turned heads.

"Come on, sug." Lil. Blessed Lil picked that moment to come striding between the desks, height augmented by a pair of very bitchy heels. His purple faux-fur and the pale pink zebra stripes across his skirt were a loud *fuck you* to the gaping cops still left on duty. The rest of the room sank into shades of gray and drab around him.

"Took you bloody long enough, Jimbo." Lil glared at Connelly, lifted his chin then looked down his nose at both cops as he brushed past them to lay a possessive hand on my arm. "Let him sign whatever he has to sign. I'm taking him home." His expression was hard, and, although his eyes flashed, the thin set of his lips, the tight ridge of his shoulders showed me he was upset.

I think everyone else took it for anger. I knew different. Still, he was there. For me.

Connelly pushed the papers and pen closer to me, then poked a finger at the dotted lines I was expected to sign. I quickly read through the document, and Connelly nodded to Lil when I was done.

Lil draped the ugly faux-fur over my quaking shoulders. "We're done here, honey." He didn't move his glare from Simpson's face as he guided me toward the front door of the building.

Not until we were past the little man and almost to the door did I speak. "Lil, where's Bri? Vic said—"

Lil tightened his lips. "Not here. Vic's in the car waiting."

"But is he okay? Did Carl... Oh, shit, Lil, what happened?"

I could tell by the way the color touched his cheeks only in high, bright spots that it was taking everything he had to keep his emotions in check. I hadn't seen him this close to losing it in a very long time. And he didn't answer me. Because he blamed me? I'd brought Carl into their lives. Lil had been adamant on keeping him out of their home. Had he gone there looking for me? Did he even know where I was? Did he care?

We didn't talk any more on the way down the front steps or across the lot to the car. He kept a hand on me, though, and it was unexpectedly comforting.

"Here we go." Lil latched on to the car door handle, and I blinked.

I'd lost a few minutes of time. It seemed I had been sitting at Connelly's desk then we were at the door, out, and now Lil was handing me into the passenger seat of the car.

"Belt up, sugar."

I reached for the buckle and winced. So much of me hurt I'd forgotten about my chafed wrists. They'd stiffened up in the cold, and I inadvertently rubbed the damaged, and now poorly bandaged, skin against my jeans.

"Ow! Shit, that hurt," I said.

"All right." Lil's voice was so soft in my ear as he reached over me to buckle my belt.

I didn't instinctively flinch this time. The belt clicked into place before he managed to touch it, though, and I glanced over.

Vic sat stiffly behind the wheel, watching me. Vic had done up my buckle, and now he leaned forward a bit and thanked Lil. "You'll meet us at mine, yeah?"

Lil nodded, even as his jaw set and his eyes flashed. I recognized the look of secretive, stubborn will I'd seen so often in him.

"Lil, follow me." Vic's voice turned stern. "Brian's safe where he is, and I want you safe too."

"I should be with him." All that stubborn defiance bled away, and Lil looked suddenly so forlorn.

What had I done? How had I got him mixed up in this shit just when he was back on track—healthy, happy?

"There's nothing you can do for him by going there alone except put yourself at risk," Vic said. "You know how he feels about this. He has protection."

Lil tightened his lips again, to a puckered white wrinkly crease. He gave a curt nod and pulled back, closing the door with a decided thump.

The car was silent for a long minute while Vic waited for Lil to get into his own vehicle then pull around to wait for Vic to lead the way.

"Vic?"

"Never would have made you for a purple leopard-print man."

"I was cold," I mumbled and scrunched deeper into the synthetic fur. The lights from Lil's car swung round to illuminate the interior. I got a good look at Vic's face. He appeared tired – his big brown eyes held worry as he gazed at me. "Warm now," I assured him.

Lil had taken care of me, and it finally sank in what a good thing Brian had.

"Good." He gave a satisfied nod and turned the key in the ignition.

"He is," I said abruptly. "Brian's a lucky man to have him."

Vic nodded. "They're lucky to have each other. Brian went through a lot to stay by his side."

"A lot of flak from me, you mean."

Vic smiled grimly. "From everyone who cared about him, I would imagine. Brian just has that kind of heart, to take it all and still stand by his man."

"What did Carl do to him, Vic?" At least he was talking about him in the present tense, so my original fears were probably unfounded. "Did he hurt him?"

Vic's assent was careful, stiff, as though the admission would somehow break him.

"Is he okay?" I pressed.

He replied with pursed lips and a curt nod. He wouldn't open his mouth after that, though, concentrating on the drive, on weaving in and out of the waning rush-hour traffic. Behind us Lil followed dutifully, and a few minutes later, both cars pulled into a small lot outside a four-apartment brick building. Vic got out then led us up the front steps into the hallway and to the number four door at the back, top of the building.

Inside, the place reflected just the same image of Vic I'd come to expect. Spare, strong, simple. Everything of the best quality, but on a cop's salary, not much of it. A leather sofa and a glass coffee table fronted a large-screen TV hanging on the brick wall. To the left was a dark wood table and two high-backed chairs. There was a tidy arrangement of three lilies in a clear glass vase on the table, which took me by surprise, but somehow seemed fitting. In the kitchen, on the right, the concrete counter held an espresso maker and a small microwave. Down the short hall, the door to what I assumed was his bedroom was closed.

It was a stark contrast to my own messy, ad-hoc place, and reflected completely different taste to Lil's flamboyant decorating strategies. It felt like the home of a man who craved sanctuary. I wondered if he often let anyone up here. I rather expected he didn't.

"Make yourselves at home." He tossed his keys into a dish on a shelf by the door and set his cell beside it. He took Lil's coat from me then removed his own.

I don't know why the sight of his gun and holster was a shock. The contrast against his white T-shirt sent a shiver down my spine, though, and I found myself moving a few feet in the opposite direction. He slipped it off. Hung the holster in the hall closet next to the coats. Tucked the gun away in a drawer, which he locked.

"You have a first-aid kit?" Lil asked, his soft voice startling me more than it should have. "Some jerk cuffed an innocent man and exacerbated his injuries."

"Lil." I automatically stepped up to defend Vic. "He was doing his job."

"It's okay, Paul." Vic sounded so tired.

I suddenly wondered just exactly what he'd had to go through in the hours I'd been holed up in that cell. "No, it isn't." My heart pounded, sending heat and jitters through my body. "None of this is okay. Lil."

"You going to step up and take responsibility for this mess?" Lil moved close, towering over me.

I couldn't tell what he was thinking or how much of it was directed at me. "I'm sorry. It's my fault—"

"Like hell." His big hand descended onto my shoulder, and I flinched. Something—anger? Disgust?—flickered in his eyes, his lips tightened, but his hand remained gentle. "Carl is a fucked-up shit. You aren't responsible for anything he does."

"I brought him into your life."

Lil barked out a small laugh. "After everything I've put people through, you don't think I deserve a little payback?"

"No." *Not like this.* I remembered Simpson's words. *'You don't sleep with shit like that and not get tainted with the stink.'* Well, maybe those hadn't been his exact words, but the sentiment was accurate. "You've put up with my nasty remarks and bad attitude longer than you should have had to." I sighed. "I can be a jerk. And Carl didn't exactly bring out the best in me." I met Lil's eye, squared my shoulders. "I'm sorry. For everything. Not just Carl. For how I treated you."

Lil shook his head. "Honey, you think I don't know why you needed to try and protect him? Brian always said you weren't really like that. I had to believe him. You stuck by him. If it had been about me, about this" — he waved a hand over himself—"you'd have buggered off, and you didn't. So." He let out a tiny huff, blinked and shook his lanky frame. "First-aid. Come on." He took my arm and firmly led me off toward the hallway.

The man had presence, and he knew when to use it. I followed, relieved enough that here, at least, were people who only wanted to help, that I didn't mind the way he ordered me about. From what I'd seen of his relationship with Brian, he was used to being obeyed, and I had no reserves left to fight him anyway.

Vic came after us, directing us into the bathroom and

handing over the first-aid kit. He didn't stick around, and Lil worked in comforting silence. The process of getting the old, bloodied bandages off and new ones applied left me giddy and lightheaded. Finally, he finished and I sat on the edge of the tub trying to find the energy to move. A minute later, it was Vic who came in to fetch me.

"All right?" He lowered himself onto the closed toilet seat and peered at me. Every movement was stiff, as though he was barely managing to hold himself together and upright.

"No." It was completely irrational to want to throw myself into his arms and hope it all went away. I wasn't sure I could deal with any of it.

He nodded. "I made soup if you're up to it."

I gazed at the new bandages around my wrists. Lil had washed away the old blood, cleaned me elbows to fingertips. It was the only part of me that didn't feel dirty and tainted.

Again, Vic nodded. "Bath first. Then food, then sleep."

I lifted my gaze to him. "You a mind reader?"

His smile, even shining through his own strain, made my breath catch. He reached out and cradled the side of my face with one hand. I vaguely wondered what his dark skin would look like against my paler, freckled cheek.

"No." He moved his thumb gently.

My eyelids fluttered involuntarily.

"Just not completely oblivious." His thumb continued lower, over my lips.

I didn't resist the urge to turn my head into his touch. I needed to ask him questions. About Brian. About how he knew so much about me. I should have been more careful. I didn't know a thing about Vic, and he seemed to know everything about me. That wasn't normal. But then, what about my life was? He offered comfort and what felt like safety. Lil trusted him enough to listen to him, and Lil didn't listen to anyone.

"Okay," he said.

He moved his hand, caressed the back of my neck, and I realized my eyes had drifted closed.

"Don't fall asleep in the tub."

I jerked upright as he reached across me, turned on the faucet then set the plug.

"I'll fetch clean clothes," he said. "Be right back."

I stood as he moved to the door. "Vic."

He turned back.

"Thank you."

After a slight pause, he lifted one shoulder in a shrug. "For what? Believing your boyfriend is a mass murderer? Stalking you? Arresting you?" He snickered, but it was just a tired, defeated sound.

"For whatever it is that makes me trust you anyway."

He nodded, and as I watched, some of the strain fell away. His eyes unshuttered. There was so much in there I didn't understand, but nothing to fear.

"I'm through letting him hurt the people I care about, Paul. Job be damned. You're more important than a badge."

"You don't even know me."

He smiled, the kind of expression aimed almost mockingly at himself. "No. But I want to." He opened the door then stepped out but turned back to me from the other side. "You okay with that?"

I think my grin came off crooked and a little idiotic. I could blame it on not much sleep, no food, on lightheaded loopiness and the complete chaos that had become my life. Or not. "I'm okay with that, yeah."

When I emerged from the bath almost an hour later, Lil sat at the kitchen table, a bowl of cooling soup in front of him. He was glaring up at Vic.

"What's going on?" I glanced between the two of them.

Vic stood with his hands on his hips, his angry expression a mask for something deeper. I could still see that glint in his eyes, too close to panic. He didn't like being out of control, and Lil was not someone who would stand for someone else taking over for him.

I backed off a step or two.

"No." Vic frowned more deeply, crossed his arms in front

of himself, and refused to let go of Lil's attention.

"What, I'm a prisoner now?"

"No. Just..." Vic sighed and slumped into the chair opposite him, deflated. "Why take the chance? For what? Pantyhose and pumps?"

"Don't mock." Lil tightened his fingers into fists, hiding his perfect manicure.

Another sigh. "I'm not mocking." Vic reached over and patted Lil's hand then got up again and headed to the stove. "I just don't think it's a good idea. In fact, I think you should just call in tomorrow and stay here. Where you're safe."

"Vic." Lil rolled his eyes. "I'm a big boy."

Vic returned, plonked another bowl of soup on the table opposite Lil, and leaned over him. "Tell me Brian didn't say the exact thing I just said when you left for work last night."

Lil snarled at him. "I don't need you to babysit me."

Vic straightened, arms crossed over his chest again and feet spread, exactly like I remember my father doing back before he fell apart, when he was trying to look stern.

"Him, on the other hand..." Lil continued, waving a hand in my direction. "He needs a good grounding. Keep him out of jail."

Heat flooded my cheeks. "Asshole." I plopped into the seat where Vic had set the soup.

"Pantywaist." Lil picked up his spoon and delicately sipped his soup.

Vic burst out laughing.

We both watched him for a minute. The aggression drained away with some of the tension from Vic's shoulders. He eased his stance and rubbed a hand over his face.

"Humor an old alpha dog, would you, Lil? At least let me take you over there. You can pick up what you need, and I'll bring you back here."

Lil rolled his eyes again, but he nodded. "Fine."

That's when Vic's cell rang. He took the call and wandered off a ways. I couldn't hear everything. I did hear a name and a lot of cursing from Vic.

"Kevin." I set my spoon down without having touched my soup. I knew I had to be pale. The room spun a bit. Kevin. That had been the name Vic muttered into his phone, as though trying to place it. I didn't have the same trouble.

"Who's Kevin?" Lil reached across the table to touch my hand.

I pulled it back into my lap. "Carl's father's name is Kevin."

From across the room, I could feel Vic's gaze on me. "Lil, I've called in a uniform to meet us at your place. I have to go in to the station. He'll bring you back here."

When Lil started to protest, Vic shook his head sharply. "Please, Lil."

Vic was staring at me, and I saw the rest of his request in his eyes. He didn't have to say it out loud.

"He doesn't want to leave me alone, Lil." A few days ago, that much over-protectiveness would have made me crazy. Now, I met Lil's gaze and only just managed not to ask him to stay and to hell with his pantyhose.

"Carl's back in action." Vic's quiet statement set my gut churning. "He's killed his father. Probably on his way back into town. I have to go."

He didn't say *I have to find him*, but it was all over his face. God, I hoped he found Carl before Carl found him.

"There's just no end to this bloody nightmare," Lil whispered.

I started shivering again.

Chapter Eleven

Carl sat outside Paul's place, drumming his fingertips on the center of the steering wheel. He'd driven from Greg's and had arrived back in town, safe under cover of darkness. For a while he'd watched. Young people occupied those homes, and any one of them could come back from a night of clubbing and spot him. An hour passed, him seeing no one, so he slipped out of the pickup and entered the building. The silence inside cloaked him, and his footsteps echoed, giving him the feeling he was the only person on the planet. Unnerved by that thought, he slid the key into the lock on Paul's front door then stepped inside. If Paul was home it meant someone else had posted bail — *probably that fucking Brian or Lil* — but if he wasn't inside...

Then my plans haven't been fucked up.

He searched the rooms, pleased at finding them all empty. In a bold move, but unable to stand not knowing for sure, he used the landline to call the police station. Disguising his voice, he inquired whether Paul was in residence there.

"Who's calling, please?" a bored-sounding desk jockey asked.

"A friend."

"And your name is?"

"Listen, is Paul Murdoch there or not?"

"Hold the line, please."

Shit.

Carl gripped the receiver then slammed it back into the cradle, the sudden thought of line tracing sending dread through him. How long had that line been open? Wasn't it thirty seconds before they could get a trace? He laughed at his stupidity. Paul's home number would have been logged right away.

Fuck!

He left the apartment, taking the stairs in a mad rush and skidding on each landing. Outside, he scanned the area, running across the grass to the pickup, head down, heart beating way too fast. Once in the driver's seat, he gunned the engine then pulled away, his destination the police station. Crazy, fucking crazy going there after that call, but he had to know. A part of him admitted something was off. Why hadn't that cop just told him whether Paul was there? All right, Paul had probably been hauled in on a murder charge—or two—but Christ, a simple yes or no wasn't too much to ask, was it?

He scrubbed his palm over his chin. Wouldn't be long before he had a full-on beard—and that wasn't a bad thing. A sense of shit having gone down gripped him, like he knew for a fact things hadn't panned out as he'd hoped. That he was being hunted. He chuckled. Was a higher calling telling him this?

Behave your fucking self. This is you, not some otherworldly entity orchestrating things. Probably instinct. Yeah, I can go with that.

At the police station, he reversed into a parking space in a line of vehicles outside. Five uniformed officers stood on the steps on a smoke break, their exhalations joining as one cloud above their heads before vanishing. A suited guy came out to join them, striking a match on a bright yellow box then lighting a cigarette.

Detective. Gotta be.

How could Carl find out what the hell was going on? He smiled as a thought snaked into his mind. Could he do it and get away with it? Nodding and adjusting his cap, he got out of the car and headed toward the cops, who looked up as he neared.

"Can y'all help me?" he drawled. "I heard my brother's in there. Think he might need bail postin'." He smiled, lips closed, keeping his eyes narrowed. "Got a call from our mama tellin' me to get my ass down here and haul that sucker out! Damn fool. Told him time and again not to steal no shit."

The suited cop crushed his cigarette beneath his heel then picked up the stub. He shook his head and returned inside, disappearing through an internal doorway.

"No one in the cells—for once. They've all been let out," said a burly uniform, smoke curling from his mouth with each word. "You sure you got the right cop shop? Might have been taken to the one in Drummington. Depends where he was picked up."

Carl slapped his thigh. "Aww, damn me! My mama said this one, but you can sure as shit say she's got it wrong." He smiled again then sighed. "Looks like I need to give her a call and find out where my bro really is, 'cause, man, she'll be frettin' until I get him out." He raised a hand in thanks and walked back to the pickup. In the driver's seat, he peered toward the steps, but the cops had gone inside.

He peeled out of his spot, wondering where Paul was. Drummington station—they wouldn't have taken him there. No, he'd be with that fucking Brian and Lil.

Probably just Lil. Too much to hope I nicked one of Brian's arteries or something.

He headed toward Brian's place, musing on whether to knock them up or just watch. He dickered between the two options for the whole drive, keeping his visual attention on the traffic, sparse as it was, in case any cops patrolled. Last thing he needed was the pickup being spotted if it had been reported as stolen. Easing the vehicle around a corner, Carl then slowed to a stop opposite Brian's apartment. He glanced up at the building, the large living room windows facing him, and the sight of a light on inside Brian's gave him hope. Maybe Paul had been released, hence someone being awake up there, or maybe that Lil was on one of his weird-ass shifts. If Paul was out of jail—if, indeed, he'd even been inside in the first place—it didn't matter.

The bail option would have worked out so well, me saving Paul and all, but I'll think of some other way to make him grateful he has me. Yeah, he'll be damn grateful by the time I'm done. No fucking doubt about that.

Someone walked past Brian's living room window. Not Brian, Lil or Paul. No, some guy Carl didn't recognize. He moved past again, phone clamped to his ear, and Carl strained to make out his features. Nothing registered as familiar, and he frowned.

Who the fuck is that? And why the hell have they got someone over in the middle of the night?

He laughed, the sound loud, startling him.

Unless they're having a gang bang. Wouldn't put it past that Lil. Weird motherfucker.

The guy didn't pass the window again, and Carl remained vigilant, gaze glued to that building, his observations rewarded when Lil approached the window then snapped the drapes shut.

Shit.

Seconds later, someone stepped through the main building doorway, and Carl hunched down in his seat. He followed the guy's progress, the shape of him shrouded by shadows, but it was the same dude from Brian's apartment. His side profile matched. The man strode to the curb behind the pickup, and Carl stared at him in his rear-view mirror. The guy unlocked a low-slung sports car then slid into the seat.

Flashy bastard.

An engine hummed then the car eased past the pickup. Carl stared inside, the sight of the driver sending him crazy with hatred.

That damn fucking guy Paul stared at a while back. What the hell is he doing round Brian's?

Anger spiking inside him, Carl followed his instincts and swerved out of his parking space, trailing the sports car far enough back that he'd appear like any other driver.

Nothing to see here, I'm just taking a night-time drive.

As their destination became apparent, Carl's guts clenched. He parked farther back than he had before, the pickup's higher seat giving him full view of the police station. The car in front had turned into the parking lot beside the building, and now the driver walked from there to the steps, engaging in conversation with yet another group of officers smoking.

Man, next they'll be breaking out the damn donuts. No wonder they can't catch me – they never do any work.

The driver nodded, patted one officer's shoulder as though he knew him well, and realization dawned.

He's a fucking cop!

Paul had to be at Brian's. No other explanation for that cop being there – unless he'd taken Brian's statement. Yeah, that had to be it. Lil would have called the cops about Carl's visit. No way would that freak keep it quiet.

Carl waited until the officers went inside before he drove away, mind awhirl with possible scenarios and how he should deal with them. Adrenaline whipped through him, chasing away any tiredness he'd usually feel in this situation where he'd had no sleep, and he found himself back outside Paul's. Scanning the street once more, he deemed it safe enough to stay. He reclined the seat, grabbed the motel blanket and pillow then settled back for the long haul.

Fifteen minutes passed. Fifteen minutes of going through his options, working out what to do next. The sky lightened a little, and he glanced at the dashboard clock. Christ, where had the time gone? Daylight would arrive shortly, revealing him to people leaving for work and maybe noticing the pickup parked outside their homes. He doubted being there would seem significant until... No, he'd covered his ass. The police weren't looking for him. That feeling of being hunted returned, though, and he shivered, mind chugging along to figure out an alternative plan. If the cops *were* onto him, did that mean Paul had dropped Carl in the shit?

If he did, it means... Fuck. I can't be without him. Won't be without him. He won't have let me down. He loves me. He just doesn't realize how much, that's all.

Another two hours slipped by, with Carl dozing, resting his eyes but his mind and ears still alert. The sound of car doors slamming brought him fully aware, and he raised the seat, longing for a coffee or cold soda to wash away the fur on his tongue. A bright burst of sunlight glanced off the windshield and he squinted, watching those leaving for work, the street emptying of vehicles until only his pickup and two other cars remained.

Further exposed, Carl pulled his cap peak down some more then glanced in the rear-view mirror. Heavy stubble covered his lower face, and he laughed. Even he didn't recognize himself. Rooting inside the glove compartment, he found a pair of sunglasses. He slipped them on, the large lenses changing his appearance further. Satisfied, he started the engine then headed out of the street and toward a convenience store a few blocks down. It served hot coffee — albeit from a vending machine — and he bought one plus a bottle of Coke and some snacks. Back in the pickup, he returned to Paul's street but parked farther down than before. Close enough to see any comings and goings but far enough away that his identity wouldn't be made out.

While sipping his coffee, he thought about Kevin. That man would be left there for days, he reckoned, body fluids seeping out of every orifice, dripping onto the floor, the stench putrid and too disgusting to breathe in for those who found him. No less than he deserved. And Greg. What about him? Carl guessed he'd be found quickly. A guy like that would have friends, family, people who'd miss him if he didn't show up for work or to a lunch appointment.

Carl switched on the radio.

Might even be on the news right now. Guy slain in kinky sex game.

Laughter huffed out of him, the bray of it quickly doused as Carl caught sight of a car drawing up to the curb. A cop car. He lowered in his seat, heart rate picking up, the coffee churning in his belly. Two officers got out then entered the building. If they'd gone to Paul's apartment they were pretty damn lax. Carl had made that call hours ago.

A few minutes later, they emerged, climbed into their car then drove away. Carl released a sigh, a stuttered exhalation that bothered him, made him wonder if he was scared without realizing it. Was he? He examined his emotions and came up with the answer that him not knowing what was going on had unsettled him. Just a bit.

Okay, more than a bit, but I've got this shit covered.

He shrugged, telling himself those cops had been there on another call, for some other reason, and he sat on, waiting, knowing Paul or Brian or Lil would arrive soon. If not today then tonight, and if not tonight, then some damn time. Coke and snacks finished throughout the course of the morning, Carl noticed the first signs of fatigue. His body ached, its heaviness preventing him from doing anything but keeping still. He moved only his eyes with each passing car and every person leaving or entering the building. Several minutes passed with him fighting to keep his eyes open, and eventually he gave in and allowed them to close, his body twitching as sleep claimed him, the last sound he registered his own breathy snore.

* * * *

A plain-clothed policeman returned with Lil less than an hour after Vic had shut the door, locking me in with an admonition to "Stay the fuck put." Even had I been inclined, I had no wheels. I was bone tired. I could barely think, let alone traipse about the city.

The cop who brought Lil back was a short, burly man with a pleasant face and a ready smile. It seemed like thick black curls covered just about every visible inch of exposed skin.

He held out one olive-skinned hand in greeting as I let them in. "Mr. Murdoch, I'm David Danforth. I'm sorry about…what happened."

"Do you believe that name?" Lil swept into the apartment loaded down with duffel bags and dragging a suitcase. "I brought your bag too, sug." He dropped my duffel at my feet and clapped his hands. "Come on, Davey Dan. Let's get this show on the road."

Lil at his finest.

"Show?" I glanced between them.

Danforth was openly gawking at Lil, who bustled about the apartment tucking his bags into a corner then examined himself in the mirror over the hearth.

"You get used to it," I assured David.

Danforth sighed. "Quite a she-devil, that one."

"You have no idea." I wondered what kind of ordeal Lil might have put the poor man through on the ride over, but he seemed solid enough. Likely, he could withstand the fire and brimstone that was Lil at the top of his game.

He shook himself slightly and pulled his attention away from the drama queen. "I have orders, Mr. Murdoch, to bring the two of you back to the station with me."

"You what? The station?" My feet moved, independently of my will, backing me farther into the flat, away from him, the door, putting Lil between us. So much for not hiding behind his petticoats.

"Relax, honey." Lil patted my shoulder, gave it a little squeeze. "They only need us to answer a few questions about that piece of filth you've been sleeping with."

Ouch.

"That's all, sir," Danforth hastily agreed.

"Um…yeah." I glanced at Lil. "Yeah. Okay. Of course." I shrugged, realized I was hugging myself so let my arms fall to my sides. "I don't really know what I can tell them they don't already know."

"Even what seems insignificant to you now might be enough to help us find him," Danforth explained.

"Besides" — Lil picked up my bag and handed it to me — "if I know Vic, and I do, he's going nuts about not having you safe and sound where he can see you and know that scumbag isn't about to jump your ass."

"Stop calling him names, Lil, please."

Lil lifted one eyebrow, studying me like he might something scraped off the bottom of one of his oh-so-fashionable pumps. He stood there a long time, arms crossed loosely over his abdomen. Finally, he tilted his head, letting out a loud sigh. "Yes, Paul, because I can definitely see your dilemma." He flipped one hand out, palm up in front of himself. "Carl." He flipped the other hand out. "Vic." He waggled them both up and down. "Vic, Carl. Carl, Vic."

"Lil—"

He took a step toward me, and for the first time ever, I felt actually threatened.

"Grow a set, Paul. For your own good." He shoved the bag into my arms then pointed one finger over my shoulder toward the bathroom. "March in there and put on your big-boy long pants. It's time to end this."

It was hard to get mad at him for being right. It was hard to get my head around Carl being what he was too. I didn't want to believe it and couldn't deny it. And I didn't want Lil to see how much that hurt.

I took the bag and retreated into the haven of Vic's bathroom, where I cowered for a good ten minutes before pulling out jeans still damp from the dryer and struggling into them. *Perfect. Clammy denim.* Just the thing for the day that had started a decade ago and didn't look to be over any time soon.

Chapter Twelve

Danforth took a convoluted route back to the station, approaching the building from the back, then spirited us inside through a dingy back hallway. There wasn't a whole lot more action in the main room when we arrived than there had been when I'd left. Thankfully, Simpson was nowhere in sight, but the way Vic squared off opposite his own partner stopped me barely inside the room. He seemed frantic.

"Please tell me you don't actually expect me to consider this," Vic spat.

Connelly shrugged. "You know it will work."

"He's a civilian."

"He's also the only one Carl will approach."

"It's dangerous. Idiotic." Vic shook his head.

"It'll work," Connelly insisted.

Vic glared him down. "No."

"The asshole stuck a knife in your partner, Vic. Watched him bleed out in a filthy alley."

Tension tightened Vic's muscles, lining his expression with steel. He just kept shaking his head.

"You know it's only a matter of time," Connelly went on. "Right now, Carl still thinks there's something there. When he finds out Paul even glanced in your general direction, how long do you think that will last? You saw what he did to his own father. What do you think he'll do —?"

"I won't let him risk his life over this!" Vic slammed a hand down on his desk.

I jumped.

"Find another way, Jim." Vic's voice went from shouting

to eerily calm. "There's always another way."

Connelly shook his head. "And how many more bodies do you want to pull out of alleys while we figure out a safer way to flush him out?"

Vic shook his head too. "It's too dangerous."

I had a sinking sensation I knew what they were discussing. I took a deep breath and stepped forward. Connelly saw me first, nodded, and sank into his chair. As soon as Vic turned around, my reluctance to insert myself into his space vanished.

"Hey." I tried a tiny smile. It bounced off his stony demeanor, and I tried a little harder. "You okay?" I gave in to the desire to touch him, to try to sooth away a wisp of the frantic energy emanating from him.

"Paul."

He reached out, and I did the only thing I could. I let him pull me over into his arms. It was just the five of us in the room, and it was nice having Vic's protectiveness covering me. He relaxed his tight hold after a few seconds. The hardness around his mouth and eyes eased.

I looked up at him and tried my best to project calm. "You want to use me as bait for Carl."

"No." His grip clamped down hard again.

"It'll work."

"You don't know that."

What was he trying to protect me from? Rejection by a psychopath?

"I know him. Whatever he's done, he's different with me," I said.

"If you say he won't hurt you, Paul, forget it. I've seen the bruises." His voice was as tight as his grip.

"I know." I could barely get my words above a whisper. "I know he has to be stopped. I know he's dangerous." I had to step back a bit to really see Vic, but I didn't get out of range of his touch. "I also know he loves me, however twisted he is about it. I know he'll come back to me if he knows where to find me."

"No."

I squared my shoulders. "Don't pull the high-handed shit with me, Vic. You want to keep me safe, figure out a way to make this work, because it's the best chance you have to catch him. As I see it, one of two things is going to happen." I couldn't quite stop the shudder at what I was about to admit, but I plowed on before Vic could get a word in. "He's going to know that I know the minute he sees me. He's going to know things are changed between us. He'll either try to kill me or he'll run. If he thinks he can't get close to me, he'll just run. He'll keep killing, and you will waste a very long time trying to catch him. That isn't how I want to see you spend your life. I want this over." I reached up to spread my hand over his chest. "I want my life back."

"You don't know what you're talking about, Paul."

"Yes, I do."

They all turned their attention to me, and I stepped away from Vic's embrace. Much as I wanted his comfort, he had to know I was not dependent on it, or him.

Lil eyed me down the bridge of his nose, arms crossed, diva-like, over his chest, his expression stony. If I hoped for support there, it didn't look like I was much likely to get it.

Connelly remained, as always, passive and difficult to read under his beard. Danforth nodded at me when I glanced at him. Strange to find support there, but welcome just the same.

Vic's eyes burned with frustration. "Paul." He stepped up, quick to close the distance I'd put between us.

"Don't, Vic." I put my hand out, not to feel his nearness this time, but to hold him off. "Don't try to talk me out of this. I know you want to protect me. You can't. It's already done. He's already destroyed everything I thought I knew." I took a deep breath and let my hand fall. I needed him to understand. "If I'm going to salvage anything that's even worth getting to know, I have to do this. I have to see it for myself. I have to see him. On his terms, and know what those terms are."

"That's as insane as he is," Vic snarled.

My faith in his reasons for trying to keep me from helping skidded. "I need to know, Vic."

"What? You need to see the crazy in his eyes up close to believe it?"

"Yes!"

"He's dangerous!"

"You think?" *Fuck! Of course he's dangerous. How did Vic imagine I didn't know this?*

He blinked big brown eyes at me, shook his head. "You don't know. You haven't seen... I can't—"

"Fuck you."

He swallowed whatever he was about to say in return, backing off as though I'd slapped him, and I hurried on before he could regroup.

"You don't know me, Vic. I'm not some virginal damsel who needs your protection. I got myself into this shit. I'll get myself out."

He closed his mouth with a snap, though his nostrils flared with his sharp, uneven breaths and he clenched his hands into fists.

"I *need* to get myself out. I let him..." I gulped in a deep breath, curled my lip at my own hesitation, but squared my shoulders once more. It wasn't like this was new information for any of them. They'd all pointed it out at one time or another. "I let Carl get away with too much. Because he was stronger than me. Not just physically, but... mentally, I don't know. I bent to what he wanted, even when I didn't want it. I will not do that again." I willed him to understand. "I will not bend, Vic. Not to him, or you, or anyone else. Ever again. This is my battle. You can't fight it for me. I won't let you."

"This is what I do. Let me—"

"No!" Why wouldn't he listen? I had a sudden flash of memory of Carl telling me what I wanted, when I knew perfectly well he was wrong, telling me he would do what he pleased to me, that I'd like it, it would be okay. It hadn't been. Nothing anyone could do would ever change that, any more than it would bring Lil's brother or any of the others back. But this, this had happened to me. I was still here, and I'd be damned if I would let anyone else tell me they knew what was best for me.

"This is my life, Vic. Let me live it."

"Or lose it?"

He was so close. I didn't remember either of us moving, but he was right in my face.

"You don't know what he's capable of," he said.

"You don't, either — not — not how he *can* be. How he was once. He didn't start out a killer!"

"But that's what he is, now, Paul. A killer. A rapist."

Blood drained out of my face to pool in a churning mess in my gut. I couldn't move.

Vic lifted my hand, held my bandaged wrist in front of my face and shook it. "Cold-blooded. Pitiless. Ruthless. Everything you're not. You can't do this."

I ripped myself free of his grip, ignoring the searing pain of opened scabs. "He won't hurt me."

Vic drew his eyebrows together. "He already has. Why can't you see?"

"I know him. I know —"

"Do you want a body count? Do you want to see the pictures? You do *not* know what he's capable of!"

"Don't I?" Frustrated, I grabbed the hem of my T-shirt and yanked it off over my head. "Look at me!"

He didn't. He pinched his lips and turned to Lil, as though hoping to find support there.

I snatched at his arm and wrenched his attention back to me. "Look at me!"

Finally, he forced his gaze down across my torso. He was about as pale as I felt.

"He did this to me." I glared at him, at his beautiful eyes focused on my bruises and full of that unnamable emotion. "He did this. He —" I snarled, and my entire body clenched with fury at him for making me say it out loud. "Okay, so maybe I didn't protest, didn't fight him off. Maybe I hid how I really felt—that I didn't want it that last time—"

Nothing.

Vic stared, pallid and angry, eyes like fire burning through the last shred of my dignity. I clenched my teeth and forced the hated words out.

"He raped me. I know. This is my life. I have to take it back."

At last, his gaze drifted up my body, across my face, and he stared into my eyes.

All that anger just bled out of me, like he'd lanced it away.

"If anything were to happen to you…"

I stepped back into his space, finding the solace I'd hoped for when I'd first come into the room. I dropped my shirt and touched his cheek. He vibrated with tension. I wished there was some way to ease his mind other than backing down.

"Just make sure nothing does," I said. "Be there. But don't deny me this. I have to take my life back, Vic. Please. Tell me you understand."

He closed his eyes, denying me that oh-so-frustrating and confusing glimpse into his thoughts. He leaned forward, and this time I didn't back away. His forehead touched mine.

"I hate that you're right," he whispered.

I ran my hand along the fuzzy hair of his arm toward his chest, closed my eyes, and basked in the sizzling strength and nearness. "I'm not particularly thrilled about it, either, believe me."

I rested my palm on one broad pec and felt his heart beating underneath. After a stretched pause, Vic covered my hand with one of his. His breath wafted warm over my face. Now I was the one vibrating. I very much wanted him to stake a claim, even though I'd just finished telling him I was my own man, even though there were people in the room with us, watching and listening. When his lips did touch mine, they weren't tentative. They didn't have the hard, bitter taint of frantic possessiveness I was used to, either. I wondered if I'd ever been kissed like that before, or if I just didn't remember.

"All right."

When we broke apart to Lil's comment, we found him waving his hand in front of his face. "Get a whiff of that testosterone. If the two of you are done with the whole horn-butting thing...?" He lifted an eyebrow at us, but the look he leveled at me was one I'd seen him give Brian when he was especially pleased with his man.

A little smile passed over my face at the thought that Lil might actually be proud of me. I guessed Carl's true personality wasn't the only one I'd come to understand through all this.

I squared my shoulders a bit and turned to Connelly. "You have a plan?"

* * * *

A loud bang startled Carl awake—so loud it sounded close. Too close. He jolted forward, gaze darting back and forth, behind and in front. A cab idled at the curb ahead, the occupants too far away for Carl to see them clearly, but something about the front passenger brought Carl's mind to full attention.

Paul stepped out onto the path, paying the driver through the window. He glanced up then down the street. He looked tired, panicked even, and rushed toward the building, turning his head left then right before he disappeared inside.

Carl's stomach muscles bunched at the sight of him, and his heart hurt. Shit, he loved him. Knew that now more than ever, the thumping of his pulse and stinging of his eyes more proof. He waited for long moments, then quickly, a surge of excitement coursing through him, Carl exited the pickup. He went inside the building. Paul would be in his apartment by now, what with the elevator indicating its descent by the glowing green triangular light on the side panel. He jabbed the button, impatient, then changed his mind and took the stairs. Tiredness fled, and he made it to Paul's door in record time, using his knuckles to rap the wood below the peephole with three short, sharp knocks.

Carl stood to the side of the door and waited.

"Who is it?" Paul asked.

Even through the door, his voice had sounded...tight.

Do I answer as me or...?

"Gas man, sir. Report of a leak in the building."

Fucking lame. Like he's going to believe—

The chain rattled, and Carl readied himself for a hasty entrance, dependent on whether Paul's features showed shock or pleasure at seeing him.

They showed wide-eyed shock. And horror. And repulsion.

Carl stuck out his foot, wedging it between the door and frame. Paul's mouth worked, but no sound came out. He widened his eyes and curled his fingers around the door edge as he tried to push it closed. Carl shoved the door, both hands flat against it, and Paul let go, staggering backward then crashing into the wall. Carl smiled, shutting the door and snapping the deadlock down and the chain across.

"Hey, baby," he said, arms out, waiting for Paul to step into them. To realize he wasn't anyone to fear but someone who loved him to distraction.

"What are you doing here?" Paul sidled along the wall, gaze darting, then dashed across the hallway and into the kitchen.

Carl rushed after him, catching Paul yanking open the utensil drawer and bringing out a knife. Paul held it before him and backed away, catching his foot on the table leg.

"What the hell's all this about?" Carl asked. This wasn't happening. He was seeing shit due to being tired. Paul wasn't standing there with a damn knife and fear plastered across his face.

"Get away from me," Paul said, knife hand shaking. "Get

the fuck away."

"Get away? Oh, yeah. We'll be getting away all right. We'll go someplace, yeah?" Carl moved forward. "Go someplace nice and quiet where no one knows us. We can start again. We don't need anyone else, do we?"

Paul frowned, swallowed hard, and shook his head. As though what Carl had said was stupid. "Start what again?"

"You do want that, right?" Carl stepped closer, knife in his peripheral vision, main gaze fixed on Paul's eyes, which flicked from side to side, stilling on the doorway behind Carl. "Ah, I see maybe you don't." Carl stifled a sigh of frustration. "Still, it doesn't matter. It's what you're going to get. We're made for each other, you know that. No point denying it."

The knife wavered, and Paul raised it, exposing his bandaged wrist. Carl lunged forward, gripping that wrist with biting fingers, digging his nails in the soft underside, twisting the bandages against what he imagined was raw skin beneath. Their gazes met, and a battle of wills ensued, one Carl knew he would win. He always won.

Paul splayed his fingers, the pain in his wrist — it had to be that — drawing a sharp gasp from him. The knife clattered to the floor, spinning across the tile then coming to rest in front of the cooker. Carl spun Paul, securing his wrists behind him, then marched him toward the bedroom, Paul struggling to get away the whole time. Paul didn't speak, instead issuing noisy exhalations that showed his anger and frustration. As they neared the foot of the bed, Paul jabbed his heel into Carl's shin. Pain bloomed there, but nothing Carl couldn't handle, and he bit back the curse tormenting his tongue. He didn't want to hit Paul, he really didn't, but he raised his fist then cracked it against the back of Paul's head. Paul yelled out, and Carl released him, flinging him onto the bed where he landed heavily with a battered grunt. Carl quickly rummaged inside the wardrobe for a belt. With Paul disoriented, he dragged him up the mattress and secured his wrists to a post, going back to the wardrobe for another belt to tie his ankles.

This wasn't what he'd intended. Wasn't how he'd envisaged it to be, but Paul needed time, that was all. He'd come around. Hadn't he always in the past?

"It's a shame I have to do this, but I need some sleep, and by the looks of things so do you."

Paul twisted and blinked at him. "Let me go."

Was he less angry? His voice had lowered, the edges of his words blurred together, like they sometimes did when he was softening to the point of truly submitting. That hadn't happened in a long time.

Carl climbed on the bed to snuggle up behind Paul, the feel of him like a balm, like he'd come home. "We'll rest a while, yeah? Then when we wake up, we can discuss where we're going. We'll be all right, so long as we've got each other, baby, you'll see."

"Carl." Paul squirmed against the tight grip of Carl's arms around his chest. "You shouldn't have come back."

"I had to. I came back for you, babe." He squeezed Paul and nuzzled his neck. "It's all been for you."

"No," Paul whispered. But he stopped squirming. Stopped trying to get away.

Carl pulled the comforter up to cover Paul and stop his hard shivering. "It'll be all right. Promise."

Chapter Thirteen

Connelly had had a plan, all right. And the second I'd laid eyes on Carl at my door, it had gone to shit. In the abstract, I maybe could have handed him over. Seeing him there, looking ragged and desperate, even for that split second before the usual mask of superiority had slammed down, I'd felt myself unraveling. I'd let him in, because that was the plan. He'd expect me to. That was also the plan. Do what he'd expect and nothing else. Don't let him get suspicious.

His short beard had thrown me off. I hadn't been able to read his face. Every time I'd opened my mouth, the wrong thing had come out. He'd just gotten edgier and edgier, and I knew what happened when he tipped over. My body still ached from the last time. I'd snapped. Plan or no plan, he wasn't going to touch me again.

Whatever had possessed me to pick up a fucking knife fled about six seconds after I'd had it in my hand. I'd have never been able to use it, and Carl knew that. He could have talked it away from me. Once, he'd been a good talker. He'd been able to talk me into just about anything. Now, he just forced the issue with pain. Whatever feelings I had left for him had crumbled apart as he'd dragged me back to the bedroom. That dissolution of my connection to him was the one thing I could never let him see. I'd seen it in his eyes—as long as he thought I loved him, he'd keep me. The minute he understood I no longer wanted him, I was nothing.

I wasn't sure when the shivering had started again. Sometime after he'd hit me and tied me, before he'd gotten into the bed too, my body just began to shake. Now, despite his arms around me, the heat of his body against my back, I couldn't stop the cold chills racing through me.

"You shouldn't have come back." *I could have kept what little of you I had left...*

He tightened his embrace.

I closed my eyes, remembering when I'd loved the feel of him holding me like this.

"I had to. I came back for you, babe." His beard scratched as he nuzzled against my neck.

I wanted us back. For that moment, before he spoke again, I wanted to go back in time, to see how to fix him before he'd turned into this...

"It was all for you."

"No." *Don't say that. Please, don't say that.* But there it was, said, and true. Somehow, I hadn't loved him hard enough or well enough, and now...

He pulled the blankets over me, wrapped himself closer around me, and I let him whisper in my ear about how it was all going to be all right. But nothing was right. I wondered if Vic and Lil realized how badly I'd failed. This entire mess, all those dead men, came down to me not being what Carl had needed me to be. Maybe he was right, and we did belong together. I couldn't imagine Vic wanting me when he figured out I'd somehow led Carl down this path.

I suddenly wished I could roll over, hold him willingly, and tell him how sorry I was. But he wouldn't let me go. And he wouldn't believe me if I told him I'd stay. It was impossible to give him what he wanted now. He wasn't stupid. He knew this was the last time for us. Didn't he? And he spent it holding me, loving me, like I hadn't felt from him in so long, instead of fucking me.

Which made me wonder where he thought we would be able to go together and remain safe. That thought catapulted me beyond shivering straight into icy terror.

What if he didn't ever expect either of us to leave this flat?

* * * *

Sleep clawed at Carl, and his voice slowed in telling Paul how their future would be. He'd already explained them being together—always—never apart with what he had in mind. They didn't need anyone else. Didn't need the trappings of life to spend eternity together. Giving up speech, he thought about what came next, but he needed a nap in order to progress to the final stage. A meal together—and if it meant Paul being manacled still, so be it—and conversation, the kind where they got everything out in the open so they could move on with a clean slate. No good harboring grudges or holding emotions inside. No, it all had to be laid out there for them both to see and deal with. It wouldn't be long and they could put this silly business behind them, go to a better place.

His body sagged into the mattress and his muscles relaxed, his mind floating at that in-between stage before sleep fully grabbed him. Paul would have plenty of time to think while Carl slept, to remember the good times they'd shared, and Carl hoped when he woke everything would be back how it was. Before life had turned to shit.

An irritating knocking jabbed at his nerves. He ignored it, thinking Paul was working to untie the belt. He wouldn't be able to—not with the way Carl had secured it—so it wasn't a problem. Except it went on for a long time, or seemed to, and a thought streaked through his mind.

The door? Someone knocking on the door?

He jerked upright, disoriented, and stared through the bedroom doorway and out into the hall. The sound came again, insistent, louder. Carl sighed and climbed off the bed, a little unsteady on his feet as he walked out of the room. He paused and glanced back at Paul, who lay with his eyes closed, chest rising and falling as though in a deep sleep. Carl longed to join him, to doze away the last few hours they had together and wake refreshed, ready to begin the new phase. He rubbed his gritty eyes, the sting of them harsh, then drew his palms down his face.

The knock came again.

Damn inconsiderate fucking jerk.

Annoyed, Carl moved to the front door. He peered through the spy hole. No one stood in the outer hallway, and he grimaced, turning to go back to the bedroom. Christ, he needed sleep badly. His body felt so heavy and his mind, though alert, wasn't firing on all cylinders. A sharp rap had him jerking around and back at the door in seconds, eye pressed to the spy hole. Still no one there. Usually, he'd have swung the door wide and given whoever hid beside the door a piece of his mind, but he couldn't be bothered. Kids, probably skipping off school, had dared one another to knock and run. Yeah, that's what it was.

Back in the bedroom, Carl got onto the bed, careful not to wake Paul, who looked so at peace, so *right*. It had been worth it, doing all…this. Risking everything to show Paul how much he cared. Not every lover killed to show their devotion. Not every lover was prepared to go to such lengths. Paul would see that once Carl explained. He'd understand why and be thankful he was adored so fiercely, then act the way he should have all this time, giving Carl what he needed inside the bedroom and out. No more resistance. No more Paul wanting things all his own way.

Carl closed his eyes, letting the pull of sleep come to take him away.

Another knock startled his eyes open.

"Right, that's it. Fucking had enough now." He jumped from the bed, lethargy gone. He stalked toward the front door. "Whoever you are, fuck off!"

Whoever it was tapped again.

Jesus fucking Christ! If I open that door…

Would he be faced with a kid or the cops? He couldn't risk seeing either. Cops being there, well, it was obvious why he couldn't answer, but a kid? Shit, he'd wring the little bastard's neck. Not something he wanted to do, not with where he and Paul were going. So far the deaths had been justified. He'd compartmentalized them away from everything else in his mind, telling himself that those he'd killed had deserved it for a variety of reasons. A kid didn't deserve what he'd dish out, and he didn't think, if Heaven really existed, God would be pleased at an unwarranted death.

He leaned on the doorjamb and positioned his mouth at the frame. "Look, we're trying to sleep in here, all right?"

Something scuffled outside — *feet shifting?* — and Carl held his breath, hoping the visitor was walking away. He moved his face to the spy hole and peered through. A guy stood on the other side, and Carl jumped back, leaning against the wall beside the door. Was it a cop? He couldn't be sure. Had the guy worn a uniform? Then again, if they were after him for murder, it stood to reason they'd send a plain-clothed officer around. Wouldn't they? And wouldn't there be more than one?

Panic slightly eased, Carl peered out again. The guy remained where he was, gaze fixed on the door, jaw muscles flexing. Tousled brown hair flopped over his forehead, and a hooked nose bore signs that the man liked a drink or two, broken red veins prominent. His hooded green eyes gave Carl the creeps, but he stayed in position. No way would some man scare him.

"What do you want?" Carl asked, his even voice belying the tremor of insecurity nestling in his gut.

"Gas leak in the building."

Carl laughed at the irony. Did everyone use that fucking excuse? "Yeah, pull the other one."

The guy lifted a small laminated card attached to a chain around his neck. "Got my identification right here, sir."

Carl examined it, unable to read it clearly, but the photograph on it matched the man. Didn't mean a damn thing, though. The police — wily bastards — were well able to create cards like that. He'd seen it on TV.

"Think I'm stupid?" Carl said, narrowing his eyes. "If there's a leak, we'll come out when I smell gas and not before. So, like I said, fuck off." He waited for the man to give up and go away.

He didn't. Lowering the card, he raised a clipboard, the paper attached complete with gas company logo. Still didn't mean anything. Anyone could mock up that kind of shit these days.

"Sir, if I could just come in to check, I'll be gone within five minutes."

The clipboard went out of sight.

"I don't think so, buddy." Carl sniffed—smelled no gas. Scrubbed his chin. Itched to grab a knife, open the door, and ram the blade into the guy's chest.

Can't. Mustn't.

He glanced back to the bedroom. Paul still slept.

"Sir, if I don't gain access to check, I'll have to call the police."

Carl returned his attention to the door. "Say what? Like they're going to be bothered about something like this!"

"Let me in. Now!"

The man's tone of voice and words sent Carl back to another time. His breath caught in his throat, and he pressed his back to the door, splaying his hands over the wood. Kevin had said the exact same thing one time when Carl had fled to his room and barricaded himself in, knowing the belt was to come.

Carl had been messing around in the lounge, kicking a ball against the wall — something Kevin wouldn't tolerate if he was in the room. Kevin was in the shower, getting ready for his weekly night out at the local bar. The ball knocked Kevin's glass of red wine onto a brand new shirt he'd laid out on the back of the sofa. Rather than wait and admit he'd done it, Carl ran to his room, dragging a set of drawers in front of the door, his chest inflating as he drew in huge gulps of air.

I'm for it. He'll see it and come get me…

The creak of the floorboards outside Carl's room indicated Kevin had left the bathroom and walked past. One of the stairs groaned under his father's weight — the fifth one down if memory served right — and Carl breathed harder, knowing Kevin would see the stain and come roaring up the stairs, irate as fuck.

He did and hammered on the door, the knob turning as he tried to gain entry. "Let me in. Now!"

Carl hunkered in the corner, wedged between the bed and the wall, knees to his chest, arms about his shins. Shaking.

"Kid, I said let me in! You ruined my shirt? Yeah, I know you did, else why can't I get in here?" A pause. "I mean it, kid. Open the fucking door!"

Carl's guts rolled over, and warm tears dribbled down his face, dripping off his jawline onto his grubby Superman T-shirt. He swiped them with the back of his hand, sick to death of living in fear, of hoping Kevin would give up and go away.

He didn't.

The chest of drawers slowly inched forward, the base scraping the floorboards, the whine it produced much like the one Carl wanted to release from his mouth. Kevin's face appeared in the partially open doorway, eyes ablaze and lips drawn back over his teeth. He'd shoved his way inside, shunting the drawers out of the way, and advanced on Carl. Shivering, Carl tried to push himself farther into the corner, wished the wall was made of fluid so he could swim to safety. Kevin reached out and gripped Carl's hair in an evil fist, then yanked the boy upright and flung him onto the bed.

"Think you could get away with that, kid?"

Kevin's red-wine breath stung Carl's eyes, and he closed them, rolling over, waiting for the inevitable.

It came swiftly, the belt's bite wicked on his ass and thighs. Carl clamped his lips closed, determined not to cry out, but the lashes gained speed, the snap of them against his body too much to handle.

His cries sounded like a wounded animal.

Carl gritted his teeth, irked that tears fell down his face, mimicking the event of years ago.

"No," Carl said to the guy outside. "Get lost."

"Well, then. I have no alternative but to—"

"I'm warning you, man. Fuck off!" Carl's words seeped

from between his clamped teeth, and he balled his hands into fists, willing himself not to give in and let the man in.

"Let him in, kid. Bet you can't face up to what you've done."

Turning, he made sure the door was secure then walked into the kitchen. Irate, he unplugged the fridge. He gripped the sides, his intention to scoot the appliance in front of the door thwarted by a loud crack. He ran into the hallway. At the door, he leaned toward the spy hole. The guy held a rammer and was in the process of swinging it back for another smack at the wood. Other men stood beside and behind him, their flak jackets evidence of who they were.

Gas man, my ass.

His anger grew and, with no time to block the entrance, Carl lunged for the bedroom, slamming the door. Uncaring whether Paul woke now, he moved to the wardrobe and slid down one side, pushing it toward the door. Sweat broke out under his arms, and his face grew hot with the exertion. Wardrobe in place, he dashed to the window to check the back of the building. No cops occupied the rear grounds, but he couldn't exit the apartment from there. He didn't want to. His plan had been to get himself and Paul somewhere no one could touch them — and that plan hadn't changed. It would have to be implemented sooner, that was all. He closed the drapes and stood beside the bed, watching Paul. Should he wake him or let him pass on oblivious?

A resounding snap rent the air, followed by the sound of the front door smacking against the hallway wall.

"Shit!" Carl whispered.

Paul opened his eyes and stared at Carl, mouth agape. "What's going on?"

Carl studied him. Paul's reaction had seemed genuine enough. "Some bastard at the door breaking in."

Paul's mouth twitched. Was that a smile trying to break out there?

No, he wouldn't find this funny. He wants to be with me as much as I want to be with him. I can see it in his eyes. See the shock. He loves me.

Carl longed to join Paul on the bed and kiss away his fears. Shouts from the hallway filled his ears, and he clamped his hands over them, humming to drown them out. Then, with an infusion of strength, he darted to the wardrobe, patting around on top until his fingers touched what he sought. He found the handle and pulled it toward him, taking the gun case down and placing it on the bed.

"What are you doing?" Paul asked, eyes wide, panic written all over his face.

"Doing what I should have done a long time ago." Carl opened the case. He removed the gun then inserted bullets with a steady hand.

"And what's that wardrobe doing there?" Paul stared from Carl to the door then back again.

"You expecting someone?" Carl asked, pointing the gun at Paul.

"No. No! I— Look, whoever it is…maybe we can get rid of them."

"Get rid of them?" Carl almost laughed. Was Paul stupid? "Not likely. They're cops. Too many of them. We haven't got enough bullets."

"What are the cops doing here?"

Carl stared at Paul. Did he know what Carl had been up to lately?

He must do. I saw that brawny cop at Brian's earlier. No fucking way Paul isn't aware of what I've done.

"They're coming for me, babe. I wanted to explain, but—"

Heavy footsteps running down the hall made Carl stop speaking, and a thump on the bedroom door jarred his last nerve.

"Police! Come out with your hands behind your head!"

"Carl, make them go away," Paul said.

"You haven't got the balls, kid."

"Shut up," Carl snarled.

"What?" Paul frowned.

"Not you. Him." Carl jerked his head to where he saw Kevin standing beside the wardrobe, smirking his head off.

"What the fuck are *you* doing here, old man?"

"Old man?" Paul echoed. "What old man?"

Carl looked at the gun, wishing he'd had time to explain, to make things right with Paul before he blew his head off.

Then swallowed a bullet himself.

But there was no time to lay it all out. All there *was* time for were the two gunshots needed to take them to the place where they'd always be together.

Carl pointed the gun at Paul. "I'll tell you everything when we get where we're going." He smiled, wishing things had been different. "I swear it."

Chapter Fourteen

I tried to sit up, remembered the bonds holding me, and shuddered back. I jerked experimentally at them, but Carl had made good work of keeping me captive.

"Carl, please." This wasn't how this was supposed to work. The police had said to let him in, to not make him suspicious. That they'd be there before Carl could do anything. But Carl had arrived too soon, and the cops had taken so long to come. Now, what was I supposed to do?

"What are you talking about?" I asked.

Carl didn't answer, just kept frowning at the gun, muttering and glancing at the door. I strained to hear Vic's voice through the hubbub, but everything was too chaotic.

"We can figure this out, Carl. Please." I twisted my head away, unable to think with the gun filling my field of vision.

"Look at me, Paul."

"Put that away. Please."

"Look at me!"

Terrified, I snapped my head around and did my best to ignore the threat pointed in my face. "Don't do this," I whispered, my voice choked with my pleading, as it too often was with him lately. "Please."

"This is the final stage. Everything I've done for you..."

"Don't make me one of them." I scooted forward as much as my tied hands would let me. If I could just touch him. Some surreal part of me needed to make sure he still had warmth in his skin.

"One of who?" Carl asked.

Outside the bedroom, cops shouted and stomped their feet. I darted my attention to the door and the dresser, but

I quickly focused back on Carl. "Those men. I'm yours, remember? You did this all..." I couldn't say it. That would make it too real. "You said we'd go someplace together."

Carl just looked at me. The gun wavered but didn't fall.

"You remember." I swallowed, tugged at my bonds again, pulled my knees up, trying to get comfortable. "Back when...when we started? It was fantastic." I managed a smile, even, and fought to ignore the commotion on the other side of the door. "You protected me from everyone."

Looking back now, I could see Carl's actions for the signs of dangerous obsession they were, but at the time it had been nice to be wanted that much.

"We were so good together, Carl."

"Were?" Carl's brow bunched in a deep frown.

"We're going to go away, remember?" I hastily reminded him. "Together. We're going to get all that back. Just you and me."

"You want that?"

"I want you to be happy, Carl. Safe and happy."

"I had to..." Carl frowned harder. "You understand, right? They were..."

"It doesn't matter now, Carl. It's over. Whatever they were, it's over now. Just you and me." I yanked at my hands again. "See?"

"You and me."

He shuffled over to the bed to flip me easily onto my back. He opened the belt holding my ankles then knelt between my legs. The gun he set down on my chest. It was surprisingly heavy, and I couldn't take my gaze off it. At least for the moment it was out of his hands. Hands that were suddenly at my crotch, popping open the button on my jeans.

Why haven't the police started coming through that door?

"Carl?" It was all I could do not to squirm.

"One last time, Paul, yeah? You and me."

"Carl." I glanced toward the door. "Get rid of them first."

"Why?"

He had my zipper open, and the beginnings of panic stirred in my gut. Why this frightened me more than having a deadly weapon pointed at my face I couldn't say. But I couldn't let him see it.

"Because they'll see me." I willed him to look at me while I could still fake sincerity enough to have him believe me. "I'm yours. No one else should see me. Make them go away."

Carl stilled his hands and stared ahead at the wall. Paul was right. He shouldn't be seen. Not by those bastards out there. They weren't worthy enough to set eyes upon him, taint him with their steely gazes. Paul was good and pure and whole. Not like *them* — those men had deserved to die. Deserved a knife to their damn throats.

Blinking, he zipped up Paul's jeans and gazed down at him.

He's my life. The one I belong with.

A loud banging smacked on the door.

And those men out there… They're in my fucking way.

Carl snatched the gun from Paul's chest, reversed off the bed on his knees then turned to face the door. No way were those fuckers going to stop what he had in mind. He teetered on what to do next as the wardrobe nudged forward and an inch gap grew between the door and the frame. Should he shoot them both before the cops came in, or get rid of them as Paul had asked? He could do that one last thing for Paul, couldn't he? Shoot the motherfuckers to kingdom come then turn the gun on Paul, with promises he would join him a second later? He nodded and raised the gun, waiting for the wardrobe to slide across the floor with the weight of the first unlucky son of a bitch to walk into the room.

His heart pounded hard and fast, and breaths rushed out of his mouth and nose. His two-hand hold on the gun remained steady, and shuffles from the bed sounded behind him. Paul hiding himself by curling his body into a

143

ball? Yes, Paul was hiding himself. He no more wanted to be seen by those men than Carl wanted him seen.

He still loves me. Shit, he understands, he really does.

A surge of confidence winged through him, and Carl watched in a surreal state of calm as the wardrobe glided in a slow-motion arc, the gap between the door and frame growing wider, wider...

A dark shape filled the space, full police gear on his bulky body, a helmet complete with lowered visor over his face. Carl tightened his finger on the trigger, and he hoped there were only six cops out there, otherwise he was fucked. Adrenaline spread through him, and he snapped his finger back. The retort of gunfire shocked him for a second, the sound ringing in his ears and paining his head. A burning sensation speared his upper arm, and he separated his hands, one still holding the gun, grasping at the air like a claw with his other. He staggered back — everything was so damn slow! — and the figure in the doorway jerked his head to the side as Carl's bullet ripped and splintered the doorframe.

I missed! I fucking missed!

His body at about a forty-five-degree angle now, Carl continued to fall back and smacked against the floor, a huge breath whooshing out of his mouth. Muffled voices — so far away, so quiet — filled the room, and he rolled onto his stomach.

"You okay, Paul?" someone shouted.

The tenor abraded Carl's nerves, the strength of the voice so loud compared to the other near-whispers. He winced, pain shooting up his arm, and he stared at the bed. At Paul, whose wide-eyed gaze was fixed on someone behind Carl.

How the fuck do they know his name?

He sighed at his stupidity.

Of course they'd know it — if they're the same cops who arrested him for murder.

"You did good," the same voice said.

He did good? What the hell?

Something pinned Carl down at his lower back.

A boot. Some bastard has his boot on me.

Realization smacked him into real time, into knowing Paul had been part of some plan to catch him.

He betrayed me. Fucking betrayed me. After all I've done for him...

Carl raised the gun, pulling back the trigger, his intent to shoot Paul so no one else could have him.

"Do it, kid. Kill him. He did good — he did good, you hear me? He's on their side not yours. He doesn't love you, and you know what you gotta do if he doesn't love you."

The gun went off a second before another boot came down on Carl's arm, holding his wrist to the floor. The boot's tread bit into his skin, and he took his gaze from Paul to watch the gun skittering across the floor. Another foot kicked it farther away — *so many legs and feet in here now* — and Carl bucked, fighting to free himself from whoever held him down.

"Cuff the bastard!" someone yelled, a new voice, louder than the previous.

Rough hands yanked Carl's arms back, the pain in his biceps so severe his head spun. The cold touch of steel encircled his wrists, the *snap* of the handcuffs extraordinarily obscene in volume, and Carl cried out. Another sharper pain swept through him, that of losing Paul, losing his control, losing every damn thing he'd worked so hard to get.

He closed his eyes as someone hauled him to his feet, unable to look at Paul or any of the men crowding the bedroom. A hand closed around his upper arm, the one that burned like a bitch, and he gritted his teeth, refusing to give them any pleasure at his pain. A jerk sent him reeling sideways and he snapped his eyes open. He clamped his lips closed to stop the bark of indignation that threatened to spill and stared at a man in the doorway. A man he'd seen before. One he hadn't wanted to see again. Black dude, all muscles and brawn, all smug grin and piercing eyes.

"Get him out of here," the guy said, hands clenching.

"Just get him the fuck away from Paul."

Carl made to glance back at the bed, but the helmeted officer shoved him forward. The black guy stepped aside, flattening himself against the hallway wall as though he was disgusted at the idea of Carl touching him. Of them sharing the same air.

In the doorway, Carl stared at him, giving a glare he hoped summed up how he felt about some cop bastard who had designs on Paul. Yeah, he had designs all right. It was plain to see, and that knowledge tromped through Carl in thick-soled boots, churning his guts. Quick-flash images of this guy touching Paul sped through Carl's mind, and he resisted walking, dragging his heels on the floor.

"Move it!" his captor said, fingers digging harder into his arm.

Gaze still on the black guy, Carl reared his head back and hawked. A glob of spittle landed on the cop's cheek, but his expression didn't change. Anger boiled inside Carl. What would it take to rile this man?

"Paul's a lousy fuck," Carl ground out, his focus fixed on the cop's eyes. "And always remember...I was there first."

The cop narrowed his eyes just a little, but it was enough of a reaction to take the edge off the ire spiraling through Carl. He smiled then laughed, throwing his head back as he was escorted down the hallway then out of the front door. The laughter kept coming, gusting out of him in the elevator, the foyer and into the air outside.

A crowd had gathered, worried residents clustered together, and they stared at Carl, some shaking their heads, others with their eyes so wide they almost bugged out of their sockets. Carl continued to laugh, the sound a comfort, the release a balm. It obliterated thoughts of what would happen next, what had been in the past, what Paul had done to him. Nothing but laughter consumed him until that voice, that hateful, awful voice penetrated the hilarity and brought him smack bang into reality.

"You're a damn failure, you know that, kid? Always knew you'd

fuck it up. You've never had the balls to see anything through to the right conclusion. Always knew best, didn't you? Always had to do it your way or not at all. And now look at you. Caught like an animal. Loser. An all-out loser, that's what you are."

Carl stumbled across the grass toward a police car, the grip on his arm tightening, burning so damn much. His laughter petered out, morphing into sobs that racked his chest. Tears fell, hot and wet and real, damn it, and he entered a cocooned state, where everything happened as though under water.

The rear police car door yawned open.

A hand covered the top of his head and pressed him into the seat.

The door closed.

As did the door to his dreams.

* * * *

The shaking started again. The belt around my wrists dug into the old wounds, and the room seemed to drop into freezing temperatures. I had seen Carl making his decision, seen it in his eyes when he'd let go of reason, and I'd felt it in my chest, the tightening bands of regret and revulsion. Not at him. Something had made him this way, and I knew it wasn't me. Something long before me. I'd had a chance to save him. I hadn't. I'd watched him lift that gun thinking I was with him, believing in him. I'd curled myself around the nausea rolling up through my gut, a coward right to the end, not even able to watch.

I'd thought, *Carl, don't. Please don't do this.*

Gunshots were loud. The sheer force of the sound had spun my head back around in time to see him fall.

Not like this.

But maybe that was better. Maybe that was the way out he'd wanted. Instinct had had me trying to get up, to go to him, then Vic had been there, peering past Carl, just watching me as Connelly had come past Carl's writhing form to the bedside.

Not dead.

I hadn't known if that was a relief or not.

"You okay, Paul?"

Connelly's voice came from somewhere beyond the rational, snapping time like an elastic band and bringing the world back into focus. I gazed past him to Vic, still silent, watching me with that now-familiar but inscrutable light in his eyes. I swallowed. Why did he just stand there? Did he know how badly I'd failed to protect Carl? Did he think I was a fool for caring at all? I couldn't read his thoughts, but he just stared, dark eyes never wavering.

"You did good, Paul," Connelly told me as he reached to undo the belt still tying me to the bed.

What the fuck did he know? I thought about Carl, the horrific, demon fight he'd put up to get free. Had he recognized him? It hadn't taken me long to place Vic in the park in the khakis and T-shirt, so Carl wouldn't forget him easily either. And my noticing Vic back then had been the last straw, the cause of the fight between me and Carl and the rough and frightening abuse that had finally made me leave. It seemed like this whole mess had started that night, though I knew that wasn't true. Vic's haunted expression as we'd driven by hadn't been the start. It had just been the tipping point.

Connelly's tentative and careful touches shot pain up my arm and time bungeed, bouncing me backward, darkening the room to the pinpoint of Carl's last attempt to own me.

I looked back to Carl in time to see his hand come up again, heavy with the weight of black metal and hatred. I half expected him to point it at Vic, and opened my mouth to warn him.

Too late.

Gunshots were loud. Bullets hurt. Even ricocheting off the bedpost and mostly missing, only passing through the flesh just above my wrist, it fucking hurt. Surprise choked off my voice.

Vic shouted. Connelly kicked at Carl's hand, then at the gun he dropped.

The gun. He fucking shot me.

"He was going to anyway," I reminded myself in a whisper.

Connelly unfastened my bonds and pressed the sheets to the free-flowing blood at my wrist.

The sound of Carl's laughter echoed through my head a long time after I couldn't logically hear it anymore.

Now that Carl was gone, Connelly backed off, leaving room for Vic on the bed next to me.

"Thanks, Chewie. Get these louts out of here, will you?" He waved vaguely around at the lingering uniformed men and perched protectively between me and them.

"He needs a bus, Vic." Connelly gripped Vic's shoulder and he squeezed.

"Yeah," Vic said. "Send them up."

Connelly sighed. "Two minutes."

"Yeah." Vic hadn't taken his eyes off me once Carl was gone. His gaze was a little unnerving.

"I'm fine," I tried to reassure him.

"You are not." Vic touched my cheek. "Did he hurt you?"

I shook my head, which made it swim, and I winced but held up my bleeding wrist. "Just a flesh wound." Even I didn't laugh at the tragic joke.

Vic just pulled me into his arms and held on. "I'm sorry. I'm so sorry you had to go through this. I'm sorry."

"Stop it." I had to push him off. "Just stop." Once free of his embrace, though, I didn't have the heart to say what I really wanted to. That it was my fault. That I hadn't been good enough for Carl. "It just happened," I said lamely.

"Paul..."

"How long?"

"How long what?"

I closed my eyes and dropped my chin to my chest so there was no chance of getting distracted by his fathomless eyes. "How long have you known about him?"

149

"I didn't know anything definite, except that you were in trouble with him. I didn't know he was our guy for sure until your credit card turned up. When the bodies started to pile up..." He shuddered and the entire bed shook.

I needed to see him again. "So why were you watching him? How did you know everything about me?"

"Gut feeling. I can't explain it. I never could, and trying would have got me a long medical leave I didn't want. If I'd been able to find a way to prove any of it, I would have. He was too careful. Until...something stressed him out. Once he snapped, I had to do something." Now he swiveled his head down and away. "I'm sorry, Paul. I was too quick to haul you in. I wanted you where you'd be safe. I—" He sighed. "I made a mess of it. I should have found the stressor, figured him out first, and I would have known not to let you do this. I would have known how close he was to snapping."

I chuckled and marveled that it didn't sound completely hysterical. "You."

"Me?"

"Yeah. You were the stressor. We drove by you in the park. He freaked out when I watched you. It was...ugly. Anyway, it doesn't matter anymore, does it?" This time, I reached up and touched *his* face, wishing I could smooth away the worry and strain. His features relaxed under my fingers. His eyes, one minute brittle and glittering, turned soft, dark, and filled with a need I understood. "I was never going to be enough. He was so broken."

Vic nodded slightly.

"I'm not like him." I shuffled forward a bit, until my thigh pressed to his knee. "He had to do it all himself, didn't he? He had to fight whatever it was all on his own. He couldn't, wouldn't tell me any of it."

"And you?"

I took a deep breath, let it out, and gave in, leaning the rest of the way until my head rested against his chest and my weight settled into his strength. "Maybe. Just not today.

There's a lot, though, Vic. Why you'd want someone as ruined as me…"

"Shhh." He ran his hand down, flat and warm over my spine. "You didn't let him ruin you. You wanted to help him, in the end. I'm not stupid. I know you think you could have done something more for him. Sometimes love just isn't enough." He leaned back a bit and lifted my chin so I was looking up at him. "Sometimes it is."

"Is it?"

The proof was in his kiss. As I sat there amidst the shattered remnants, guilt churning my gut into a nauseated mass, he didn't demand anything. He didn't want anything but my permission, and when I nodded and his lips touched mine, it was the most natural thing in the world to lean on him and let him take all that away, even just for that moment in time.

Sometimes, the moment that changes your life is dramatic and tragic and filled with gunfire and blood. And sometimes, it's a glimpse of a face through a car window, something you almost miss, something that couldn't possibly mean anything at all.

Epilogue

I watched Brian limp to Lil's side and the familiar twist of guilt stabbed at me, even through the layers of safety and cottony understanding the two of them and Vic had swathed me in over the past months. It didn't always show, this remnant of Carl. Only when it rained and Brian remembered the scrape of Carl's knife. He twisted a bit and stretched, and patted Lil's arm when his lover reached to steady him.

"Fuck off," Brian said good-naturedly.

Lil stuck out his tongue.

"We'll see you at the pool tomorrow, yeah?" Brian asked, turning to look at me where I was still ensconced on the couch with Vic wrapped around me.

"Yeah." I got up from the warm haven of Vic's arms then walked them to the door.

"And don't forget you have to meet me right afterward," Lil warned.

I nodded even as a fair amount of heat drained from the room and I shivered.

"This is a good thing you're doing, Paul. You need it as much as these kids do." Lil rubbed a hand up and down my arm. "And I'll be there."

"You offering your petticoats to hide in again?" I asked.

"No." He actually pulled me into a hug and spoke over my head. "No more hiding. That's what this is all about. You share your story, and teach them it isn't their fault."

"I know." I'd dropped my voice to a whisper.

Lil tightened his arms fiercely. "It isn't." He pushed me away from him, still gripping my shoulders and glaring into my eyes. "You're going to say it over and over again until you believe it. Carl made his own choices. Whatever he thought his reasons were, he made his own choices."

"I know." I pushed Lil's hands away and backed up a few feet. "I know."

"Lil." Brian's warning voice sifted through the growing buzz in my ears, and Vic's warm bulk loomed behind me.

"I'm fine." A firm shake of my head dislodged the fuzzy filter, but I still backed up to prop myself against the doorframe, settling the solid wood between my shoulder blades. "Public speaking," I said lamely, even though we all knew that wasn't the issue.

Lil took a moment to smooth non-existent wrinkles out of his skirt before fixing me with that intense, no-nonsense look of his. "I know what I'm talking about."

"You've been there. It works. You can't stay silent forever," I parroted his litany of justification at him.

"Until you say it out loud, you can always find a reason to believe it wasn't what it was, that it didn't happen, that it was your fault, or a dozen other things to keep it from being real." He glanced over at Vic then back at me. "Until you call it what it is, there's always the chance it will happen again. Your father, then Carl." His lips twitched into a half smile. "You lucked out with Vic, but these kids, they might not be so lucky. They need to know it's safe to say it out loud, to look at it, see it for what it is and know how to avoid it."

"Stop it." I pushed off the wall and squared my shoulders. "I'll be there. I'll do it. I don't have to like it."

"But you do have to believe in it," Vic said from where he perched on the edge of the hall table. "They'll know, when you get up there and say 'he did this to me, and I didn't deserve it', if you actually believe what you're saying."

"Both of you. Just stop."

Brian shuffled over and pulled me into a tight bear hug. For a fractured second, I needed him off me, then it passed and I returned the embrace.

"Just tell them the truth, Pauly," he said. "Easy."

"Fuck you."

"In your dreams."

"Let's go, Bri." Lil snapped a slap across Brian's ass that made him yelp, and tossed me a mock glare.

I grinned. "Better go before Grizzelda over there starts frothing at the mouth."

"Mmm." Brian sauntered out of the door. "I love it when you get all possessive." He winked at Lil.

"Of course you do."

Their banter trailed off down the hallway, and it was the best unspoken advice they could give. I closed the door behind them then turned to Vic.

"Dishes?" I asked.

His gaze drifted over me, flicked to the kitchen then back to me. A little shrug lifted one shoulder and he smiled. "They aren't going to crawl away in the night." He held out a hand.

I watched the way his muscles rippled ever so slightly and his fingers curved into a relaxed invitation. How many times had he offered that hand, and I gave nothing but a smile in return? Not that we hadn't been together over the past eight months, but the number of times I accepted that offer were far outweighed by the times I hadn't. When I studied his face, I could see he didn't expect me to accept now, either.

"Why are you with me, Vic?"

He slowly dropped his hand back to his side. "It isn't obvious?" he asked gently.

I shook my head, having the hardest time not wrapping my arms about myself. There was a block I couldn't get past. I stood there, cold and vaguely frightened while he offered all the warmth and safety a body could want. So why couldn't I just accept it?

"At first, when you didn't even know I existed, it was because you needed my protection. You didn't know you needed it, and there was no way I could do anything about it, but I could see it. And when you did see me" — he shivered and lowered himself onto the arm of the couch — "that evening in the park, you looked right at me, like you'd suddenly found something, and I knew." He shrugged, and the motion gave him a fleeting aura of helplessness. "Why do you stay?"

It's safe.

And it was that, but seeing into him, seeing his heart and soul right there in his eyes, just for me, I had to admit there was more to it. "How long would you wait?" I asked.

His frown was puzzled, and horror raced through me when I realized I'd asked that out loud.

"There is no waiting," he said simply. "It isn't about waiting to get what I want. I have what I want. There's nothing to wait for."

"But I haven't — We haven't..." I clamped my jaw shut.

In eight months, he'd settled for kisses and caresses and cuddling and never asked for anything I didn't offer.

He lifted his shoulder again then let it drop. Standing, he held out his hand. "Love isn't all about sex, Paul."

This time, I bypassed his hand entirely and settled against the warmth of his body. His arms folded obligingly around me.

"What Lil said about making it real." I leaned a little to stare up at him. "Saying it out loud."

"You don't have to talk about anything — "

"I love you."

His mouth clamped shut, and he looked into my eyes for a long moment.

I squeezed him tight, trying to meld my body into his. "This is what I want to be real. You. Me. Us."

He floated one of his big hands over my back. The other he sank into my hair and pressed my head to his chest.

"Solid enough for you?" he asked gruffly.

I nodded, pressed into him, and twined my arms around his waist, telling myself I didn't need to hear the words back. He'd done nothing but prove how he felt for months now. It was time I reciprocated, and for once, the thought didn't bring a host of gut-churning insecurities along with it. A few minutes of standing like that separated the disappointment from the next step, and I was nearly ready to move when he did.

He lifted his hands to cup my head and tilt my face. I flowed with his movement, wanting his touch, still feeling the contrast between the dry, calloused warmth of his skin and the hard, demanding memory of Carl's. I wondered vaguely, as his lips brushed mine, if that contrast would ever fade.

His kiss curled my toes. It always did, but it was different this time. The spring-like tension I'd grown used to, the compacted awareness that allowed him to pull away if he detected the slightest hesitation on my part, wasn't there. He'd committed this time, and when his tongue swiped across my lips, I opened. Immediately, he filled my mouth with the warmth and goodness I hadn't quite admitted I was craving.

I groaned, and the pressure of his hands and his kiss intensified.

I searched up under his shirt for more of that warmth, and his breath hitched when I found skin with my cold fingers. I pulled him closer.

"Air," he rasped, after what felt like forever and wasn't nearly long enough.

"And here I thought the lightheadedness was all you." I continued to rove my hands over his back as he chuckled, and the laughter vibrated against my chest and tingled through my palms.

He pressed his lips to my hair. "Mmm."

This was a new sensation—that I could make him speechless had my heart fluttering in odd ways and prompted me to see if I could do it again. I pushed my hands up until he had no choice but to let me remove his T-shirt. Acres of dark, smooth skin spread before me. He was just tall enough that my lips came even with his collarbone when we stood straight, and I'd already discovered how easy it was to make him swear simply by applying my teeth lightly along the delicate skin there. And this time, I was not going to leave him wanting.

By the time I'd traveled the length from his left shoulder to the little divot between the bones, he was breathing hard and moaning, tangling his fingers in my hair. Clipped curses dropped off his lips.

"Bed," he said.

It was a command, albeit a whispered one, and I took a moment to suckle his throat and decide how I felt about it. The moment stretched a little too long, and he tugged at my hair, lifting my head.

The pain wasn't intense. Just there. My breathing stalled, and I tightened my fingers on his back. It took a heartbeat, and a good look into his deep eyes, to identify the scorching sensation racing through my gut as desire, not fear.

"Bed," he repeated, a little louder. "Now." He dug his fingers into the back of my skull until his lips were crushed over mine again, and desire raged into a full-blown hard-on and consuming need.

I stumbled a bit when he turned me around, propelling me gently but firmly toward the hallway and the bedroom at the end of it.

He nudged the door closed with a foot as we entered, already turning me back for another kiss. One hand left me for long enough to flip on the light switch.

"I want to see you naked," he said, gaze raking down my body. He pressed a hand to the bulge between my legs and squeezed.

"Angh... Vic."

"Naked."

I nodded and yanked my sweater over my head then tossed it on the floor.

He watched it fall, and I made a motion to pick it up. He hated mess. For him, I could be not messy.

He clamped a hand around my wrist, though, drawing

my attention back to him. He had huge hands.

"Naked."

"'Kay." My heart hammered as I fumbled one-handed with my belt, and my fingers slipped on the cold steel of the buckle.

"Scared?" His voice had lost the hard edge of command, but he still watched me, his stare intense and unrelenting.

I paused for a breath, considering the question. "No." The flutter of haste and breathlessness wasn't fear. Not with him. Not this time.

Finally, the intensity broke and he smiled. "Good."

A firm shove sent me back onto the bed and I grunted, but he didn't give me time to find my balance, just shoved again, sprawling me onto my back so he could climb on top of me. As his weight settled over me, I let out a breath and spread a hand on his broad chest, following the line of contrast between my pale skin and his dark with my gaze.

"You know what I want?" he asked as his hips ground into mine in a slow, steady rhythm.

"To make me come in my pants?"

He blinked, laughed, then kissed me. "No. Well, maybe." He smoothed his hand up my chest, lingering over my pecs and nipples, and watched its progress as he talked. "I want to make love to you. A long, slow fuck, watch the way your skin turns pink, and listen to you mutter."

"I do not mutter...oh...*fuck*."

He was sucking on one nipple and grinding me into the mattress with the pressure of his hips. His cock slid along mine as he gently undulated his body. Even through our clothes, the heat and pressure were enough to make me groan.

"Vic. Fuck. Stop." I was too close. "Don't...stop. Don't stop."

But then he eased off enough to reach between us and unbutton my jeans.

"That was you not muttering?" he asked.

I blushed.

"Yeah. That right there." He took another long, slow kiss as he pushed at my jeans to get them down past my hips and off my ass. He stopped when they were halfway down my thighs, unable to reach to push them the rest of the way. His weight and the rough scrape of denim over my bare cock, my own jeans trapping my legs, jolted me out of the moment.

"Paul?"

"No, it's—" I swallowed, met his gaze, and watched the concern chase away the desire. "I'm okay. It's okay." I was going to get past this. "Do something for me?"

"Anything." He trailed his fingers down my cheek then across my lips, distracting me enough so I focused on that light touch and not the roiling, unpleasant memories.

I wiggled until I had my hands and arms free and stretched over my head.

He narrowed his eyes slightly. "Is this some sort of test?"

"For me, not you."

"I don't—"

"Please. Vic, just do it. Hold them."

For a long moment, he studied me. "Why do you want to do this?"

"Because I used to like it," I confessed. "I just—" How did I explain? I wanted to be me again. Not a victim. "I want to know."

"I won't hurt you."

"I know." I smiled. Or tried to. "I'm not asking you to. Just hold me."

Finally, he shifted so he straddled my thighs and leaned forward to grip both my wrists in one big hand.

I strained, testing the conviction of his hold, and he tightened his grip. Every nerve in my body lit up. My chest tightened until I was panting, and still he just sat there, staring down at me.

"What now?" he asked.

I squirmed, feeling the friction of denim on skin, and my cock twitched. "What do you usually do with naked men under you?" The humor fell a little flat. I could tell he was worried, and I tried to bring him back. "Touch me."

He tilted his head and broke eye contact to take in the rest of me. "Naked men this gorgeous?" He glanced up and grinned a slightly sharp, hungry grin. "I tend to devour them."

Heat rippled through me and I groaned, tried to lift my hips then my head, reaching for him as he sat there and watched me struggle.

"Where to start," he murmured, shifting with my movements, but easily compensating, as though my attempts were inconsequential to him getting what he wanted. He had the air of someone who'd played Dom before and knew how.

"You like it too." Tension I hadn't realized was there melted away inside. I squirmed more vigorously, tried harder to get at him somehow, and he finally took action, separating my arms to take one wrist in each hand so he had a balance point to lean forward.

When he kissed me this time, there was no hint of hesitation, no holding back. It was possessive and hard, and every bit as aggressive as Carl had ever been, with one difference. He was giving me what I'd asked for. What I wanted, and not taking anything I didn't want to give.

Within seconds, my struggles ceased and the heat between us melted me into submission. He let go with one of his hands to yank at his jeans. His weight shifted, the kiss got messy as he kicked and shoved at the constricting fabric, then his hand was back, pulling mine down to his groin and the length of his hard dick.

"Lube," he muttered through the kisses. And once again, he let me go to find it.

The warmth of his body as he got off the bed left, but the heat remained as I watched him saunter over to the nightstand to retrieve the tube. He knew he was built and gorgeous, and he knew I wanted him. He played the aggressive, in-charge top very, very well.

When he came back, he stood over me where I was still lying on the bed, grinned, and quickly divested me of the remainder of my clothing. He didn't disguise the hunger in his eyes now, and when he tilted his head, I knew exactly what he wanted. I lifted my knees and let them drop open. Exposure under that kind of scrutiny was nerve-racking. He just licked his lips and smiled that same, predatory smile, sending my blood pressure through the roof.

For a minute, he stood there, watching me, stroking himself, and saying nothing.

"What?" I whispered.

He opened the lube then squeezed some onto his fingers, and again tilted his head. "You want me to fuck that?"

I nodded, my heart seemingly trapped in my throat, making words impossible. I reached down, cupped my balls and lifted, mostly just to have *someone* touching me. His eyes glittered, he curled his lips into a smug smile, and heat crept up my neck into my cheeks.

He came closer, finally, one knee on the bed, and leaned down, face close to mine, closing his free hand over my wrist again. "That's a very tiny hole, and I have a very big cock."

Shit, the things he says to me…

"Yeah," I said.

His lips traveled over my jaw, my throat, chin—I lost track as he sent me spinning.

"Lots of prep work," he whispered.

"Ye—ssss."

He slid his finger in without warning, the lube cold, the stretch tingling up through my gut and down through my legs. Another finger followed close and fast, and I hissed again as my eyes watered.

"Ahh…fuck."

"Too much?" His lips were close to my ear, sending goosebumps racing down to meet the tingle of pain.

He moved his fingers, in and out, and I groaned.

"More," I said.

"Tough guy."

"'S'good."

"My cock is going to be a big stretch, Paul," he warned, rather unnecessarily.

I'd seen it. He wasn't just bragging.

"Want it."

"I know you do."

He continued to work on me with his lips and fingers. My skin lit on fire, and I squirmed, bucking into his touch, trying to get some friction on my cock.

He pressed his hips down, rubbing his long shaft against mine. "Ready?"

"Uh-huh." One good thing about my getting shot and his being a cop. Lots of blood tests, lots of proof we were both healthy, and no need for even the thin barrier of latex. I spread a little wider for him and held his gaze while he pushed into me.

He was careful, doling out the burn in tolerable doses until he was well seated, propped on his elbows over me and looking down into my face. "Fuck me, you're tight."

I laughed. More of the tension flowed away, and his grin answered my mood.

"That is a big cock." I wiggled a bit, to better feel the fullness inside, the stretch, and his weight.

The light in his eyes danced as he wagged his hips back and forth in answer to my movement, and we both started to giggle stupidly.

Free of all the constraints now, both physically and emotionally, I wrapped my arms and legs around him, pressing myself up so my cock dug into his stomach.

"I do love you," I said. It didn't matter if he said it back. Some people didn't say it. "Now move."

He did. Slowly, methodically, stroking his hands through my hair, his weight grounding me. It wasn't long before the pace quickened, though, and he was thrusting harder, faster, and he stopped his stroking fingers, gripped, their tips pressing my scalp. He dipped his chin, his face nestling the side of my neck as his hips pistoned.

I didn't think he knew he was about to come. Some garbled, tangled words exploded from about mid-chest range, and he stiffened, every muscle locked tight, his arms squeezing the breath out of me. I heard a tiny whimper from where his face pressed to my neck, and he began to shudder, coming down from a climax so intense he couldn't even lift his head.

I stroked his hair and waited until his breathing returned, not to normal, but at least stable enough to allow oxygen to his brain.

"You okay?" I asked.

For a long minute, he lay there, heavy and unmoving.

"Vic?"

He sniffled. "Wanted that a long time," he said, face still averted. "Didn't think..."

"Vic—"

"Didn't think you'd let me," he said over my attempts to soothe him.

"Well, shit."

A soggy gurgle of a laugh issued from him, but he still didn't look up.

I let him stay there and silently stroked his hair, one leg still slung over his hip, and waited. It was a long wait. At first I kept quiet, waiting for him to say something, some big revelation, but apparently, he'd said all he had to. And it was okay. He wasn't a big talker. He'd demonstrated how he felt more than adequately over the past eight months, always being there, giving me a home, moving my stuff from my flat when I couldn't bring myself to even go into the building, and never asking anything of me but that I not hide from him.

It had been a struggle for me to be honest about the guilt and the anger. Fear was easy to admit to, and so were the memories. I'd not wanted to admit how furious I was at Carl, how horrible I'd felt as the truth about his past slowly had come out, or how much it had hurt when the cops had come one day to tell us he'd gotten in one prison fight too many. One he couldn't win. Hell. Vic had even come to help me bury him.

No. He didn't have to say a word. I knew how he felt.

"Hey." Vic's voice pulled me back to the present, and I tried to get a look at him, lying half on top of me, his head resting on my chest. "I guess that was a bit of a dud for you, huh?" He grazed a hand over my flaccid cock.

"No. It was perfect." I pulled him tighter to me and kissed his hair. "I'll just put it in the bank."

"I could —"

I shook my head. "Just hold me. I need to sleep. Tomorrow's going to be hard enough without me staying up all night getting pounded into the mattress."

He grinned, but his eyes stayed serious as he smiled up at me and stroked my cheek. "If you're not ready, no one will think less of you. It doesn't have to be tomorrow."

"It has to be sometime, Vic. Lil's right. I need it as much as the kids do. It'll help."

He nodded. "Get some sleep, then." He shifted around until I was comfortably snuggled against him, my head on his shoulder and our legs tangled together.

"Someone should turn off the light," I mumbled.

"Yeah."

It was still on when I fell asleep.

* * * *

I'd somehow pictured a sea of upturned faces awaiting my every word, a bunch of teenagers itching to soak up my misery and horror and toss it back in jibes and sneering. I wasn't prepared for a small room down the hall from the pool with a handful of frightened children needing someone to tell them it was going to be okay.

"Shit. Lil—" I turned back from the doorway, but Lil blocked my path.

"Just go inside. I'll introduce you. Whatever happens,

happens. Answer their questions."

He gave me a spin and a little shove, and I stumbled into the room.

Everyone turned around to look at me.

"Hey." I lifted a hand, smiled feebly.

No one spoke.

Lil bustled in behind me and clapped his hands. "All right. Listen up. This is Paul." He grabbed a chair from a nearby table and spun it around to face the small circle. "Sit."

Someone giggled nervously.

I sat.

"Paul?" Lil motioned to the group. "You're here to talk to them?"

I nodded. "Hi."

Lil rolled his eyes and shook his head.

"Am I late?"

Vic's deep, soothing voice rolled over me. I turned, and he grinned at me.

"I'm not? Good." He got his own chair, set it behind mine, and draped an arm over my shoulders. He leaned forward so our faces were side by side. "Hi." His gaze traveled around the circle. "Name's Vic. I'm moral support."

I gripped the hand hanging over my shoulder. Tight.

"Are you his boyfriend?"

I wasn't sure which kid asked, but Vic just nodded. "I am."

"You have a boyfriend?" This from a girl across from me. "Do you have sex?"

"Uh…" I glanced at Lil, who shrugged.

"Do you?" he asked, the question matter-of-fact and bare.

"Yes," Vic answered for me. "Now we do, yes."

"Weren't you scared?" The girl's gaze bored into me, waiting. "You know, when that mad guy…"

"Umm. I—"

Vic squeezed my hand.

"I was," I said at last, glancing at Vic. "Yeah. I was. For a long time."

Vic squeezed my hand again.

No. He didn't have to say a word.

Tools of Justice

Excerpt

Chapter One

Barry floated a bit, on drink or desire, not quite connected to himself as his lover laid the tie over his closed eyes and tied it. "Really?" A bit of his hair caught in the knot, and he squirmed.

"Really. Trust me." A tongue slicked over his ear, and the squirm turned to reaching.

He should recognise the voice, thought maybe he did. Something shifted. A scent, making him think of blood or rust, drifted by like cigarette smoke. He stood still — nude, blind and bound — and the voice chuckled softly.

"Ready, baby?"

He nodded, straining to find the familiar — so close he could almost reach a name, a face…something he knew. The hands that had tied his behind him, lowered him until his chest rested on something hard under an inadequate layer of padding.

"Relax."

Easier said than done. Barry let out a breath.

"It isn't going to hurt. Promise."

"Tag?"

"Shhh." *A hand ran through his hair.*

Had Barry caught the scent of Old Spice? The particular drag of Tag's bad leg?

"What's next, Tag? Tell me."

"You'll see."

There was a sound behind him – shuffling, grunting – then frigid air engulfed him. He shivered, glanced over his shoulder as though his covered eyes could make out what was going on.

"What?"

The hands that touched him next weren't Tag's. They were too rough, too demanding, and he flinched, made a move to stand. The hands pushed him back.

"Tag?"

"Shh." *The sound seemed so far away, too little for comfort or reassurance.*

Cold air swirled around him. He struggled to stand, but whoever held him was too strong.

"Don't. Tag, don't go!" *Panic squeezed out rational thought, and he strained. The only answer was a tighter grip on the back of his neck and one of those rough hands running up the inside of his thigh.* "Tag!"

The hand moved to clamp over his mouth, leaving him struggling for air. His bare feet on the cold cement chilled him, toes ineffectual claws, gripping nothing. No more floating. Only shivering, cold, and a gag – its straps cutting into his cheeks – and no idea how it had got there. The ball clogged his words, turned his begging to garbled, tear-washed nothing. He shouted inarticulate sounds no one was going to hear. Struggling only earned him bruises and didn't stop the invasion of those rough fingers or the wave of pain from being stretched too far, too fast.

The hand came back, around the front of his neck this time.

This wasn't how it was supposed to be. Not how he wanted to go – bound and gagged and fucked, for Tag to find his body like that.

Blackness darker than the blindfold sucked him under…

He awoke screaming.

He always awoke screaming. His voice had gone raw from it, and he only barely remembered the terror that haunted the dark. He glared at the obnoxious red glow of the clock. Not quite five. His gaze shifted to the bottle distorting the numbers, but, for once, he turned away from it, untangled himself from the sweaty sheets, and shuffled off to the bathroom.

* * * *

An hour later, a good portion of the tar-like station coffee he'd tried to pour himself landed on the table beside his chipped mug. He sopped it up with the last of the napkins and tossed the sloppy mess into the trashcan. What was left of it, he took to his desk. It might taste like all hell, but it would scour the fuzz off his tongue. The computer hummed when he turned it on, the sound a comfort in the dim stillness of the deserted police station. Maybe he could get a few reports finished before his shift started. Better paperwork than the four walls of his empty apartment.

He wasn't sure how long the screen had been staring back at him, or how long the flying toasters had been careening around the black void, when he blinked back from his stupor.

"Hey, Wiki."

He jumped at his partner's hot breath on the back of his neck.

"Still daydreaming about Tag banging you within an inch of your life?" He thumped Barry on both arms.

The coffee cup slipped from Barry's grasp. The last few, cold sips dashed out across his desk and spattered the screen, the keyboard, and his pants.

Ross snickered and plopped down in his seat across from Barry. A glare only quieted the man's mirth — it didn't banish it.

"Fuck off."

"Hey. I tease because I care."

Barry relegated his response to single digit sign language.

"Seriously, dude. You have got to move on." Ross shook his head and jabbed at the ON button of his monitor. "That ship has sailed, man."

"Sank, more like," Barry muttered, conceding to truth.

"Whittaker!" Captain Taggart's voice sliced through the room, and Barry winced. "My office."

"Used to like the sound of that," he murmured as he gave his splattered khakis one last dab and rose. Ross didn't snicker this time, and Barry patted his shoulder as he passed. "Just call me Davey Jones."

A memory of his latest dream shuddered through him as his fingers curled around the door handle to Tag's office. He was already in a cold sweat when he stepped inside and pulled the door closed behind him. It was impossible to meet his captain's eye with the irrational thoughts of blame, completely unearned, grinding through him.

"Wiki?"

Barry's head popped up from where he'd been studying a dried splash of coffee on the linoleum.

"You okay? You look like—"

"Fine. What'd you want?"

Tag frowned.

"Sir."

A heavy sigh filled the room and settled around them.

Tag finally retrieved a folder from his desk. "New case." He handed it to Barry. "Dead guy, missing girl."

Barry took the folder, flipped it open, glad for the new focus. "Do we like her for it?"

"Doubt it. Little thing like that?" Tag shook his head.

Barry understood the comment when he saw the pictures of the victim.

"Beaten to a bloody pulp," Tag confirmed, as if the visual wasn't enough. "Garrotted. Missing woman's about five foot two, ninety pounds on a rainy day. She didn't do that."

"Who did?"

Tag's eyebrows went up. "That would be the case, wouldn't it?"

"And no idea where she is now?"

"If I had to guess? Run. Whoever did this had to be one scary son of a bitch."

Barry nodded, gaze still skimming the file. "I know this guy."

Tag nodded. "Reporter. Calvin Landry, wrote for some local rumour rag." He poked at another, much thicker file still sitting on his desk, flipped the folder open, and picked up a picture, which he handed to Barry. "He was following this case. Pain in the ass, but not a bad guy. This was the last murder he ran a story on. That girl there" —he tapped the picture of a gagged and bound woman lying lifeless on a cold, cement floor in what looked to be a garage—"looks an awful lot like Calvin's girlfriend. Now he's dead, his girlfriend is fuck knows where, and I don't like where this is going one bit. If Calvin pissed this guy off, and this kind of girl is his type…"

Barry stared at the photo of the dead girl. She was young, had been pretty. He handed it back to Tag.

"She was raped—"

"Strangled," Barry whispered.

"That was COD, yeah…"

Tag's voice faded out behind the whirlwind of violent memory. Barry shook. Papers drifted down around him. "You were there."

Tag shuffled forward, his bum foot slapping awkwardly on the linoleum.

Barry started and looked up.

"I went to the scene, yes." Tag paused. "Barry?"

Barry stared at him, a bit of shellshock still ricocheting around in his head, making it hard to focus, impossible to speak.

"You had a dream," Tag said.

171

Barry didn't have to answer.

"I'm giving this to Cornwall and Riggs. Go home. Get some sleep."

"Fuck you." Barry dropped to one knee and scooped the papers back into their folder. "You have to let me do this."

"You can barely focus. You're too close. Those dreams —"

"Make me the perfect candidate to find her."

Tag was shaking his head already, though. "I know what those dreams do to you, Barry."

"No, you don't." Barry leaned in to his face, tapped him on the chest with the corner of the folder. "You left."

Tag backed off and sank onto the edge of his desk. At least he didn't argue that point.

"I don't know where they come from, or why I have them, Tag, but you have to let me use them," Barry insisted.

"What they do to you, though…"

"They do whether I use them or ignore them. If something good can come…"

Captain Taggart nodded. "But if I think you're in trouble, I'm pulling you."

Barry scooped the fat file off his boss's desk and turned to the door. "I'll find her, Tag."

* * * *

Black shadows flitted around Barry. Every time they stopped there was pain, but they never slowed enough for him to strike back or even defend himself. Every time they connected, they left a part of him broken and bleeding until he was a quivering heap of helplessness on the cold floor. The screaming and begging in the background was endless.

Then came the garrotte. Knowing it was a dream didn't make it any better…

More books from
Pride Publishing

Book two in The Dreaming series

*Just when they thought the nightmares couldn't get worse,
they realized they weren't sleeping.*

Finding a killer isn't easy, but someone's got to do it…

Book two in the Tales from Rainbow Alley series

All his life, Rory Sanders just wanted please the people he loves and always thought he failed, until the day Gabriel Stark rescues him from Kane's abusive hands.

Book one in the Voices series

Getting calls from the dead in the middle of the night isn't Oliver's idea of fun...

About the Authors

Sarah Masters

Sarah Masters is a multi-published author in three pen names writing several genres. She lives with her husband, youngest daughter, and a cat in England. She writes at weekends and is a cover artist/head of art in her day job. In another life she was an editor. Her other pen names are Natalie Dae and Geraldine O'Hara.

Sarah also co-authors with Jaime Samms, and as Natalie Dae she co-authors with Lily Harlem under the name Harlem Dae.

Jaime Samms

Jaime writes, romance, fantasy, urban fantasy, shifter stories about men, about life, about love. Her work is populated with mostly men, most of whom are into each other, and yes, we do mean into each other. You can find plenty of free reading on her website.She also reviews for Dark Diva Reviews, mostly the same types of stories, and will happily spout her opinion on the books she reads to her kids, who she home schools. Finally, she's occasionally gainfully employed. She writes for the love it, and hopes to pass on that love to her readers, her kids, and anyone else who comes along.

Our authors love to hear from readers. You can find contact information, website details and an author profile page at https://www.pride-publishing.com/